Alegra felt his lips, his heat, the hardness of his body against hers

Almost of their own volition, her arms rose and slipped around Joe's neck. She moved closer to him and felt his strength as his arms closed around her. In the next heartbeat she experienced the strange feeling of coming back to something.

He'd said she had more reasons to be here than the ones she'd given him. She could have sworn he'd been wrong, but now she wasn't so sure.

It felt like a homecoming, a returning—but that made no sense, not any more than her next thought.

That maybe he was the one she'd come back for.

Dear Reader,

Going home means different things to different people, and "going home" to Shelter Island in Puget Sound, an island that still holds the legacy of Bartholomew Grace, who was an infamous pirate from the past, is totally different for Alegra Reynolds and Joe Lawrence.

Alegra goes back home to prove that a small child who was ridiculed and pitied has become a success beyond anyone's imagination.

Going home to the island for Joe Lawrence is leaving his position as the editor of a major New York daily, and a life that has lost most of its meaning, to return to his roots and make a life for his son and himself.

When Alegra meets Joe, she thinks he's a failure, that he's given up everything she's worked so hard to get herself, and Joe thinks that she's so much like the way he used to be that it's almost painful for him to watch. Neither one knows that their lives will change irrevocably when they start to fall in love and find that lost part of themselves in the other person. They'll discover that "home" isn't a physical location but the place where love binds people together forever.

I hope you enjoy the first book of the SHELTER ISLAND STORIES, and watch for the other two stories in the series—*Home to the Doctor* and *Home for a Hero*.

Mary Anne Wilson

Alegra's Homecoming

MARY ANNE WILSON

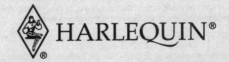

TORONTO • NEW YORK • LONDON
AMSTERDAM • PARIS • SYDNEY • HAMBURG
STOCKHOLM • ATHENS • TOKYO • MILAN • MADRID
PRAGUE • WARSAW • BUDAPEST • AUCKLAND

ISBN-13: 978-0-373-75168-6
ISBN-10:   0-373-75168-0

ALEGRA'S HOMECOMING

www.eHarlequin.com

Printed in U.S.A.

ABOUT THE AUTHOR

Mary Anne Wilson is a Canadian transplanted to Southern California, where she lives with her husband, three children and an assortment of animals. She knew she wanted to write romances when she found herself "rewriting" the great stories in literature, such as *A Tale of Two Cities*, to give them "happy endings." Over her long career she's published more than thirty romances, had her books on bestseller lists, been nominated for Reviewer's Choice Awards and received a career nomination in Romantic Suspense. She's looking forward to her next thirty books.

Books by Mary Anne Wilson

HARLEQUIN AMERICAN ROMANCE

For Joanine
Hold on to your dreams and don't let go.
You deserve every good thing. Love you lots!

Prologue

November—The Bounty Festival
Shelter Island, Washington

The pirate slipped into the crowd attending the last day of the Bounty Festival and no one noticed. Of course, every third person who attended the week-long celebration that commemorated the pirate Bartholomew Grace's historic return from his summer of pillaging and plundering in the South Pacific, was dressed like a pirate. So one more didn't stand out.

Ten-year-old Alegra moved through the throng, paying little attention to the parade that was almost done moving up the main street of the town of Shelter Bay. Other years she'd ignored the festival, but this year, after her father had brought home a pirate costume, complete with a hat, full-sleeved black leggings and plastic boots, she'd decided to walk the mile from her home in the center of the island and see what was going on.

No one gave her more than a passing glance. The hat

was too big, riding low on her face, but that was fine by her. She trudged along the wooden boardwalk of the town, passing familiar stores and seeing people she'd known all her life mingling with the strangers who took the ferry from the mainland to attend the festival.

An announcement about music at the square in town where the statue of old Bartholomew stood watch was made over a loudspeaker, but before she could head in that direction, someone stepped right in front of her. As she pushed her hat back and looked up, her heart sank.

The one person she didn't want to see was blocking her path, his band of cohorts with him. "Oh, it's little Al Peterson," Sean Payne drawled.

Sean was two years older than she was and one of the island kids who enjoyed taunting her, never letting her forget who she was. Alegra Peterson, the daughter of a man who was drunk more than he was sober and a woman who'd walked out five years ago and never come back.

In the failing light, she stared up at him. Tall and skinny, he was in costume, too, but a far more elegant version than hers, with a billowing silk shirt, high leather boots with shiny buckles and a long white plume of a feather stuck rakishly in his hat. His narrow face was pale, the freckles that went along with his blond-red hair standing out starkly on skin that was just starting to get the first traces of teenaged acne.

His gaze traveled over her, too, then his dark eyes met hers. "Some costume, Al," he said. "What're you supposed to be?"

"A pirate," she said.

"I don't *think* so," he said mockingly.

"I *am* a pirate," she said emphatically, lifting her chin and standing her ground. She wasn't going to cry and run away. She'd done that once, and it had only made Sean and his friends make fun of that, too.

"No, you're a garbage picker." Sean moved closer.

Kids had taunted Alegra for as long as she could remember, but Sean was different. To the others, she was an afterthought. To Sean, she was a target. Now he reached out and grabbed her arm, leaning down until his face was in hers.

"Garbage picker," he sneered. "That's a costume my dad threw out because it was a mess. He put it in the trash bin behind his office, right near the Ship's Rail Bar."

She hadn't questioned where her dad had found the costume for her to wear. He'd just said that it fell in his lap. Now she knew. She also knew her face was flaming, and she hated her dad and Sean in equal measure.

"So, you or that drunk dad of yours had to be garbage picking to get it," Sean continued. "Trash for trash."

She was aware of everyone watching them and listening, even passersby, and anger raged through her. She narrowed her eyes and hissed back at him loud enough for everyone to hear, "I'd rather wear a stupid old costume than have zits all over my face."

"Ooohhh," rose in a chorus from his pals, and it was Sean's turn to grow beet-red, which made his blemishes even more vivid. The instant he let her go and raised his hand, she made fists and held them up the way her dad had shown her boxers fought. "Come on, come on," she yelled at Sean. "Hit a girl. Just try and I'll beat you up."

But Sean didn't get a chance to do anything. Someone else was there, an adult who had the boy by the arm, pulling him back and putting his tall, solid body between the two youngsters. Alegra grabbed at the man's jacket, trying to get him out of her way, and the next thing she knew, his other hand gripped her shoulder and held fast. "Hey, calm down," he said.

That was when she looked up and recognized an islander, Mr. Lawrence. His son was in high school. Ignoring Sean's shouts of outrage, he crouched and fixed his dark blue gaze on Alegra. "Aren't you Peterson's girl?"

She refused to answer. He was looking at her with the same expression most of the town used. She wasn't sure what to call it, but she knew how it made her feel. "Are you okay?" he asked.

She'd never been okay, and as long as she was on this island, she never would be. She jerked and must have caught him by surprise, because she was free. Without missing a beat, she turned and ran blindly away from both him and Sean, ignoring the shouts of anger when she bumped into people. She finally broke free of the crowd and, breathing hard, kept on going.

She ran into the night, through the darkness where huge pines canopied overhead, blotting out any light that might have come from the rising moon. But she didn't need light to know where she was or where she was going. She reached the old lighthouse—out of commission for as long as she could remember—skirted the fence around it, then scrambled down rough stone steps to the beach below. She stopped at the water's edge.

Fog was rolling in over the dark waters of Puget Sound, blotting out the distant lights of Seattle. Alegra pulled off the boots and stripped off everything down to the jeans and thermal shirt she'd worn under the costume. Then she picked up the costume pieces and waded into the chilly water, not stopping until she was up to her thighs and shivering cold. She dropped the pieces into the shallow waves.

She waded back to shore and headed to a huge rock embedded in the bluffs below the lighthouse and scrambled up onto it. She sat as far back as she could, still shaking from the cold, but not caring. "I hate you all," she screamed. And then she cried.

No one heard her sobs or the moment when they stopped. Why weren't there still pirates like Bartholomew Grace? Why couldn't she stow away on his ship and sail away? Why couldn't she pillage and plunder with him, until she came back here fabulously rich? She'd throw the money in their faces and if anyone so much as called her *Al,* she'd make him walk the plank.

She liked that idea very much. And before she nudged an offender into the briny deep, she'd make him bow to her and call her *Alegra.*

"I am Alegra," she called into the fog, and heard a vague, muffled echo come back to her. "Alegra," she said more softly, alone in her world.

Chapter One

Eighteen years later

"I am Alegra," the woman said softly to herself.

She stood at the railing of the lumbering car ferry as it broke free of the docking area to make the trip across Puget Sound to Shelter Island. She stared at the distant dark blur of the island that was all but lost in the mists of the late-November day. "I *am* Alegra," she said again.

The cold dampness brushed her skin, and she pulled her cashmere jacket more tightly around her. Tucking her chin into the faux fur collar, she never took her eyes off her destination. The island certainly didn't look welcoming. She was the only one at the rail, the other passengers opting to stay in the warmth of their vehicles, but then again, they weren't coming back here after ten years. They were mostly commuters who were just going home. She wasn't.

She heard the muffled chimes of her cell phone and reached into her jacket pocket for it. Flipping it open, she glanced at the caller ID, then said into the mouthpiece, "Hey, Roz, what's wrong now?"

Her assistant, Roz Quinlan, said brightly, "Calm down. All's clear on the Alegra's Closet front, or as clear as it can be at this time of year."

The upcoming holidays increased the sales of their product—women's intimate apparel—at their stores and through the mail. Nothing was simple with her business this time of year, but it kept going. So if Roz's call wasn't a business problem, what was it? She had no family, and her friends were all involved in the company. "Did you call just to hear my voice?" she asked.

"Not even close. It's Beach Boy Ken."

Alegra grimaced. Roz didn't like Ken Barstow, the junior partner in the law firm Alegra's Closet Inc. used, and although she was polite to him, when she spoke about him to Alegra, Ken became "Beach Boy Ken." When Roz first met him, saw his tall, blond, tanned good looks and pronounced ingratiating manner, she'd decided he was "plastic and phony."

"What about Ken?" Alegra asked.

"He's been calling and leaving messages on your cell, he told me, and you haven't picked up or returned his calls."

Alegra had dated Ken Barstow off and on for almost a year, but whatever he'd thought might come from it was fading fast. She was too busy with her company to have time for a serious relationship, which in fact was the way it had been since she'd left Shelter Island. College had taken up four years of her life, design school a few more years, then there were the years spent getting her business up and running.

And, she hated to admit it, but Roz was partially right about Ken. He wasn't plastic and phony, but he was on the fast track and doing everything he had to do to further his ambition. Sort of the way she was, she conceded to no one but herself. And she'd been pulling back ever since. "Tell him I'm swamped and I'll contact him as soon as I can."

"You got it," Roz replied, then added, "So where are you now?"

"On the ferry," Alegra said as the outline of the island became clearer, and she could see the ribbon of beach below the towering bluffs, a pale strip between the dark water and the darker land. Now she could even see lights from houses twinkling to life in the coming dusk. And there, silhouetted against the darkening sky, was the old lighthouse. She felt a knot grip her stomach at the sight.

"Well, good luck to you," Roz said, which only made the discomfort in Alegra's middle worse.

Roz had been with Alegra since the day her lingerie designs first went into production. She'd been there when the first Alegra's Closet had opened in New York, and stuck with Alegra all through the struggles to get going and expand. Roz was as close as a sister in some ways, but even she didn't know everything about Alegra's past, just a general impression that it wasn't great and that she was going back to her childhood home to settle a problem before she headed back to San Francisco.

Alegra cleared her throat before she murmured, "Thanks," and flipped the phone shut.

She narrowed her eyes on the lighthouse, standing like a dark sentinel on the northern end of the island. Suddenly the past two weeks of checking on stores in California, Oregon and now Washington, seemed like another life. All the years she'd been gone were merely a blink in time.

She found herself gripping the railing with both hands, so tightly that her fingers whitened. She was back to the day, after her high school graduation, she'd packed a bag and finally had made her escape. She'd walked the two miles to the ferry landing in the pale light of a June morning, taken the ferry away from the island and found a new life. Now the old life was rushing up to meet her.

She took a deep breath, reminding herself of the reason she was coming here: the need to put Al Peterson to rest. But now that she was getting closer and closer to the island, her eyes started to burn, then her lashes became damp. "Damn it," she muttered and swiped at her tears. She never cried. She wouldn't cry. And, as her stomach began to churn, she vowed she wouldn't throw up, either.

She closed her eyes as she pressed her hand to her middle. She breathed deeply a few times and the urge to be sick subsided, though she still felt a bit nauseated.

"You shouldn't stand out here on the deck when it's this rough and this cold," a masculine voice said by her right side.

Her eyes flew open and she turned to see the man who had spoken to her. The first thing she noticed were his eyes, a deep, true blue. He was tall, over six feet, dressed in what she used to call "island traditional." That meant a flannel shirt, jeans, the more faded the better, and heavy boots. His dark hair, touched with gray at the temples, didn't look styled at all. He wore it straight back from his angular face, longer than was fashionable, and now it was ruffled in the breeze off the water. The shadow of a new beard roughened a strong jaw, and grudgingly she had to admit that he was attractive enough to catch any woman's attention. That sexy outdoorsman look...

"Excuse me?" she asked when she realized she'd been staring.

He leaned on the rail with his right arm and narrowed those blues eyes on her. "Are you seasick?"

That did away with having to explain why she'd started to cry. "A bit," she confessed.

He shook his head. "That's a shame. But it takes a while to get your sea legs."

Her only response was a small smile. She turned back to the view of the island. The ferry was about halfway there now, and she was able to see the outline of the huge pines on the ridges and the stark rocks in the bluffs.

"At least the trip's short," he said.

It felt like an eternity since she'd driven her rental car onto the deck of the ferry to begin the journey back. "Thank goodness," she breathed.

She thought he'd leave, that if she didn't say any more, he'd drift off and leave her alone. But he didn't.

Instead, he leaned forward with both arms on the rail and stared down into the dark water. "Twenty-two minutes," he said.

She frowned in confusion. "What?"

"The trip, it takes twenty-two minutes, if the weather's good and the water's smooth. If the weather's like this, and the water's choppy, it can take half an hour."

She shifted to look at him. "And you know this because you're a regular on this run?"

He cast her a slanted look. "A regular? I was, way back. I've only taken the trip a few times lately, though." He turned toward her and tucked the tips of his fingers in the pockets of his worn jeans. "But some things never change."

"You're from the island?" she asked, already knowing the answer.

A rueful smile tugged at his lips. "Yeah, I've only been back there a few months, but I guess once an islander, always an islander."

"If you say so," she murmured as her stomach churned anew.

"And you're here for the Bounty Festival?"

You're going there for revenge? She remembered Roz saying in disbelief when she'd told her the reason she was coming back: she was going to show the people who'd pitied little Al Peterson and made her life miserable that the little girl was gone, that she was now Alegra Reynolds—she'd taken her grandmother's surname—successful designer and businesswoman.

She'd denied Roz's accusation

Roz had studied her and finally said, "Honey,

success is the best revenge." But unless they knew who Alegra Reynolds was, they'd never realize how far Al Peterson had come.

"So *are* you here for the festival?" he repeated.

"Isn't everyone?" she asked.

"Well, not always," he responded. "Some come over to visit friends and relatives."

"I have no friends or any family on the island," she said, and hoped her tone sounded normal.

"A true tourist?"

She shrugged and the fur on her collar brushed her chin. "Just curious," she murmured.

Her phone rang and she opened it to see Roz's number on the readout again. She hit the "ignore" button, just as another spasm of nausea clutched at her stomach. She hugged her arms around her middle and bent forward to try to minimize the discomfort. "Damn it," she said.

She felt a hand on her shoulder. "Are you okay?"

Simple words. Yet they echoed in her mind, bouncing off the past, and pulling a day from eighteen years ago right into the present. She made herself look up. He still held her shoulder, and his head was cocked to one side, those blue eyes intently surveying her. The festival, Sean taunting her, humiliating her, then Mr. Lawrence standing between her and Sean, holding both of them back, his hand on her shoulder, him leaning over, looking at her intently, asking, *"Are you okay?"*

Just like this stranger, but he was leaner and darker than Mr. Lawrence had been back then, maybe younger.

Around forty or so, and Mr. Lawrence had been…well, to a child, old, maybe fifty. But the tone of the voice and those blue eyes, along with the strong hand on her shoulder, confused her. If she narrowed her eyes, blurred her vision, it could have been Mr. Lawrence talking to her. She shook her head to clear her thoughts, then straightened up. Thankfully he let go of her. She grabbed the rail with her left hand and exhaled. "I'm fine. It's just so rough. The water and the wind and the cold."

"This is actually pretty nice for this time of year," he said, and she knew it was true. "I've always thought it was crazy to have the festival in November. But it was November when Bartholomew Grace got back here safely from his pillaging and plundering, and celebrated. So who's going to go against the tradition set up by one of the most feared pirates who ever sailed the seven seas?" The man grinned at Alegra, obviously enjoying his little explanation. "His ghost would rise up and make us all walk the plank if we dared to mess with his plans."

Pirates and ghosts, her wishing she could have gone on a pirate ship and gotten rich, then come back and made anyone who called her Al Peterson walk the plank. The past was alive around her, and her mind raced. Mr. Lawrence had a son. The boy had been in high school or maybe he'd just graduated and gone off to college around the time of Alegra's run-in with Sean. She couldn't remember much about the Lawrence kid, since he was so far ahead of her in school, but she thought his name had been Joe.

"The old guy loved the celebration as much as he

loved the pirating, from all accounts. It was a debauchery, to all intents and purposes. Now it's a week
full of art shows, crafts, wine tasting, sailing on the
sound, parties and a parade, all topped off by a charity
ball on the final evening. Not quite the definition of
debauchery." He went on as if reciting directly from
a book. "A debauchery is a wild gathering involving
excessive drinking and promiscuity. From what I've
seen over the years, the label 'festival' is definitely
more fitting. A festival is an occasion for feasting or
celebration."

She smiled weakly. "Is your middle name 'dictionary'?"

"No, my middle name is Preston. Joseph Preston
Lawrence."

JOE LAWRENCE watched the blond woman as he told her
his name. He wasn't sure what he'd expected when he
stated all three names to her, but it certainly wasn't to
see those finely etched cheeks blush or those deep
amber eyes widen. She recognized his name? That
shouldn't have surprised him, although being on the
island for six months and being out of the limelight had
certainly lessened the chances of anyone knowing him,
other than the islanders he saw day in and day out. And
none of them were too impressed by Joey Lawrence.

Her tongue touched her pale pink lips, before she
simply said, "Oh."

"And you're…?"

She stared at him, as if he was suddenly speaking a

foreign language, then she swallowed and softly cleared her throat. "Alegra Reynolds."

Joe had spotted her at the booth where the ferry tickets were bought before they'd boarded for the trip to the island. She'd stood out in the sea of commuters getting on the ferry's last run before it shut down for the night. Her clothes had certainly made her conspicuous: the thigh-length jacket with what he'd guess was politically correct faux fur at the collar and cuffs, to the pencil-legged jeans, and the narrow high-heeled boots.

He'd watched her get her ticket, then climb into the car, a sleek black sedan, in front of his old truck. He'd guessed she was in her late twenties, with shoulder-length hair the color of rich cream, and a profile that hinted at a delicate beauty he wouldn't have minded seeing full face. But she was in the car with its tinted windows, and out of sight by the time the ferry started loading.

He'd been behind her on the deck, letting the truck idle to keep the heater going, and watched her exit her car. No islander would leave the comfort of his or her vehicle to stand at the rail and stare out at the dark waters of the sound. He'd watched her until she disappeared, then decided to go belowdecks to the small concession for some hot coffee.

He'd been up since four that morning, taking the earliest ferry to Seattle, and he was starting to feel the effects of a long day in the city. But before he'd reached the stairs that led belowdecks, he'd passed the woman and heard her mutter, "Damn it all," in a choked voice. He'd turned and she was there, looking decidedly green around the gills. He hadn't thought twice about going closer and asking her if she was okay.

Now he was standing facing her, seeing she was as beautiful as he'd thought she was. Alegra Reynolds. The name rang a bell, but before he could get a handle on where he'd heard it, her cell phone rang again.

After reading the LED screen, she answered it. As he turned to look past them at the dock coming closer and closer, he heard her say, "What now, Roz?" Then a long silence before he heard, "Do it. Let me know when the tax attorney gets back to you." As he glanced back at her, he saw her end the call, but still keep the phone in her hand. "Business," she said.

"I assumed as much. 'Tax attorney' doesn't usually come up in everyday conversations with friends and family."

She smiled softly, another expression that was so damned endearing it made his breath catch. "No, it doesn't," she said. "You lived here before and then came back?"

He nodded. "Right."

"You commute to work now?"

Despite her blush when he'd told her his name, she apparently didn't have a clue who Joseph Lawrence was. "No, I *work* on the island. I'm a writer for the newspaper, the *Beacon*—it's a small weekly for the island. We cover big stories like announcing the best peach preserves and counting the times the local drunk is locked up."

A spasm crossed her face and he was certain she was

going to be sick, but she only exhaled. "You're a reporter for the paper?" she asked.

He nodded. "A reporter and the owner."

He could tell that surprised her. "Really?"

"That's what it says on the flag, owner and editor, at least it has for the past six months. The previous owner, Clive Orr, retired to Florida to sun and fun."

"Smart man," she murmured as the wind picked up, bringing cutting cold with it.

When her phone rang again, he heard himself asking, "Does it ever stop?"

She took the device out, saw the LED and hit a button that shut off the ring. "When I turn it off." She kept it in one hand, and tried futilely to get her hair under control and behind her ears. "It's business. You know how that is."

He had a flashback to his other life, before he came home to Shelter Island. Back then cell phones had been his lifelines. Heck, he'd had three. One for business. One for personal calls. And one with a number he only gave a select few. He'd had an earpiece he never took out of his ear while he was awake. Now he still had a cell phone, but seldom turned it on, and truthfully wasn't at all sure where it was right now. "It can eat up your life, can't it?" he said.

She took him off guard when she asked, "Why did you leave the island?"

He shrugged. "You know, the old I'm-going-to-conquer-the-world attitude?"

"And you didn't?"

"I got close, then came back here," he said, not about to go into details of the twenty years he'd lived away from the island, or why he'd come back here six months ago with his three-year-old son, Alex, to make a life for the two of them where his own had begun.

The ferry slowed even more, and an announcement came over the loudspeaker. "Sorry, folks, we've got a bit of a problem docking, and it'll take a few minutes."

"Riding the ferry can be an adventure," he said as the big vessel lurched to a complete stop.

Alegra grabbed the railing to brace herself. "This could be a huge story for your paper," she said.

"I guess so," he said, aware of more than a hint of sarcasm in her tone. It hit a nerve. "Not like gang shootings or bodies in the Hudson, though."

That made her smile. "Yeah, not exactly the big, bad city."

"Alegra Reynolds. You're from New York."

It was a statement, not a question, and he could tell it surprised her. "Yes, but how—?"

"The boutique. The one near downtown Manhattan. All black and silver, with headless mannequins in the windows?" He'd gone past that upscale store when he'd walked to work instead of taking a cab. He'd glanced at it more then once, and wondered how anyone could call those tiny pieces of silk and lace clothing. "You're *that* Alegra."

She looked pleased that he knew of her. "You got it right, but how could you?"

"In my other life, I worked at one of the big New York

dailies, and our offices were about two blocks south of where your store is. I went past it a lot."

Her smile slipped, and her mouth formed a perfect *O* before she finally said, "J. P. Lawrence? You're *that* Lawrence?"

He nodded. "Used to be."

"But now you're here?" She waved vaguely to the island nearby.

"Yeah, I'm here."

"But you…" She bit her lip, looking as if he'd said he was from Pluto but chose to live on Mars. She looked stunned. "You were the editor, weren't you?"

The ferry lurched forward again and the voice came over the speaker. "We'll be docking in five minutes. Please be ready to disembark."

"We need to go to our cars."

It was as if he hadn't spoken. "What are you doing here running a weekly newspaper?"

So many had asked him that, and so many had gotten his stock answer. "I'm here for my son, to let him grow up where I did." But a part of him wanted to tell her something that was more truthful than the first statement. "I told you I went off to conquer the world, but what I didn't say was, it wasn't worth it."

She stared at him, then a frown grew. "Oh," she said. "I understand."

"What do you understand?"

"Nothing, I'm sure it's personal. Things happen, and—"

"Oh, no, I wasn't a drunk or druggie and lost it all.

No." He stood straighter. "I didn't have a breakdown or punch the publisher in the face."

She held up both hands, palms out to him, shaking her head. "No, I didn't mean that."

He looked at her hands, the long, slender fingers, and realized something. She wasn't holding her phone any longer. He didn't remember her putting it in her pocket, either, though maybe she had. "Your phone?" he asked.

She felt in her pocket, then looked back at him. "Oh, no!"

Alegra must have dropped it when the ferry lurched. They both dropped to a crouch to search.

Chapter Two

"There it is," Alegra gasped, spying it under the railing within an inch of the edge of the deck. She made a grab for it at the same time Joe did. There was a tangle of fingers, and then, as if in slow motion, Alegra saw her phone skitter to the edge and over.

She straightened, grabbed the railing and looked down into the churning water. "Great, just great," she muttered. "It's got all of my contacts in it, and my calendar and..." She couldn't stop a huge sigh. "Everything."

"It sounds as if it's your lifeline."

That about said it all, she thought, but simply closed her eyes to try to regroup. Ever since she'd decided to return to Shelter Island, nothing had gone right. Her flight out of San Francisco had been cancelled, her luggage had been routed to Salt Lake City instead of Seattle. Now her phone. She should have let this place die out of her memories and never looked back.

"Is there a cell phone store on the island?" she asked.

"I really don't know," Joe said. He was frowning.

"Why don't you just let it die a natural death and take a break from it all for a while? Just think, no interruptions, no calls when you don't want them. It could be a good experience."

He might have left his life behind in New York, but she didn't want to. "That's not a choice for me. I have things I need to take care of and—"

"And you're totally indispensable?"

Why did he make that sound so bad? "Right now, I am."

"That's quite a load to bear," he murmured, and for a crazy moment she wondered if that was pity she saw in his eyes. Though why this man should look at her with pity made no sense.

"It's business. That's not always fun and games."

"Why did you come for the festival if you have such pressing business matters?" he asked.

He'd find out soon enough on the last night at the masquerade ball on what was left of the Bartholomew Grace estate. Maybe he'd cover it for his little newspaper. It would all be over for her then, and she could leave the island behind once and for all. "I can mix business and pleasure, despite the old taboos about it."

"Good for you," he said, but he didn't sound congratulatory at all.

She suddenly felt their conversation had taken a turn into something combative. "Are you the welcoming committee, cross-examining people who come for the festival?"

She thought her words hit their mark, but the next moment, he was almost smiling at her. "Now there's a job that could be interesting, interrogating lovely ladies on the ferry."

She wasn't ready to laugh with him, and her phone having gone to a watery grave only added to the tension of returning to Shelter Island. "Now there's an employment opportunity that would beat the heck out of doing stories on peach picking or drunks."

She hated the sarcasm in her tone, but couldn't help it. This man was starting to annoy her.

"I'll pass," he said, and now she felt a chill between them. "And good luck finding a cell phone store."

"Thanks," she said. The silence that fell between them was beyond awkward. Before she turned and went back to her rental car, she found herself saying, "As far as doing business goes, I was told that you had fax machines, Internet connections and phone lines on the island."

"Thanks for filling me in. Now we can put away the hammer and chisel and the slabs of stone we use to write our stories for the paper."

She flushed, and then the bell sounded to let the passengers know they had to get back in their vehicles to disembark. She started to walk off.

"Can I ask you something before we climb in our vehicles and ride off into the night?" he asked.

She felt herself bracing. "What?"

"It came across the wires just a week ago about you coming to the West Coast because you were merging with a competitor."

She never would have guessed that a story like that would end up in the offices of a small weekly paper.

"We're buying them out, not merging. They'll become one of our Alegra's Closet stores."

His next question was unexpected. "Are you here to open a new store on the island?"

She almost laughed out loud at the absurdity of his question, but simply shook her head. "No, definitely not. I have other things to do, not the least of which is looking for some art at the local galleries."

He studied her for a moment, then said, "Nice meeting you."

"Sure," she said as she heard car engines starting, sending a low roar into the cold air over the sound of the idling engine of the ferry. She called out, "Goodbye," and headed for her car.

"Goodbye," she heard him yell after her.

She got into her rental, and as she settled, she glanced in the rearview mirror. She saw Joe open the door to a beat-up pickup truck parked right behind her. He caught her eye in the reflection, lifted a hand in a wave and climbed into the truck. J. P. Lawrence, now known as Joe Lawrence. "How the mighty have fallen," she said to herself. She wasn't sure she bought the reason he'd given—that he was here for his son. Why would anyone want their kid to grow up on Shelter Island?

JOE DROVE HIS OLD TRUCK off the ferry and onto the gravel of the landing right behind Alegra's sleek black sedan. When he'd come back to the island with Alex, he'd bought the truck from his father, instead of having his car from New York shipped out. The pickup didn't look like much, but everything worked. Besides, the Jaguar would have been totally impractical for use on the island.

As he watched Alegra inch out of the parking area behind the other cars, he thought about what he'd heard about her founding a string of high-end boutiques that sold intimate apparel on the East Coast, then setting up franchises across the country. It was a fast rise for any business, and seemed only set to grow more.

He followed her car past a small cluster of service buildings, then up the steep driveway to the highway that ran around the perimeter of the island. Most of the cars crested the rise and funneled north, and as they did, one by one, they turned off, heading for their respective homes.

He didn't turn and neither did Alegra. He thought about the cell phone falling overboard and her horrified reaction. He would have laughed if she hadn't looked so stricken. Those amber eyes had been filled with anger, frustration—and a touch of sadness.

He hadn't expected that, not when she seemed to be so successful. But then again, he knew someone could have great business success, but be totally lacking in a life beyond that. He had been a prime example of that in his other life. He shrugged that off as they entered the town, passing under the banner hung high above the road proclaiming Ahoy And Welcome To Any And All Who Enter. The Gothic lettering had a skull and cross-bones on either side.

With the festival so close, the main street of Shelter

Bay was fully festooned with wood and brass everywhere, street signs all displaying a Jolly Roger overlaying a silhouette of the island, and pirates aplenty in windows and on signs. The park at the center of town, laid out on a piece of land that jutted out toward the sound, had its huge pavilion decorated to look like a huge crow's nest on a galleon. The lush grassy area, rimmed by wind-twisted trees and bushes, was being filled with booths and food areas, in preparation for the mainlanders who would descend on the island in two days. A life-sized brass sculpture of old Bartholomew Grace, complete with raised sword and a patch over one eye, which had been donated by members of the Grace family still on the island, stood at the entry to the park.

The sedan in front of him slowed just after the park, and the right turn signal came on. Alegra Reynolds was going to the most expensive and exclusive bed-and-breakfast on the island, the Snug Harbor Cottages. A fully restored, three-story Victorian was the original building, and it fronted a series of luxurious cottages built out on the bluffs. Immaculate rose gardens separated the cottages, and strategically placed trees and shrubs added to the sense of privacy in each.

Joe had intended to keep going, but instead he pulled into the lot behind her, slipping into the parking spot next to hers. She got out when he did, and he could see that she'd confined her hair in a clip at the base of her neck sometime during the drive. The style served to emphasize her elegant features and huge amber eyes.

"Hey, there," he called. "I just remembered something." She waited for him by the door to her car. "There's a store farther down the street on the right as you go north. It's called Farrow Place. It's a secondhand store, mostly, a consignment sort of arrangement. Earl Money owns it, and he's the original diversifier around here." Joe held up a hand when he saw her frown. "I know, I know, that's not a word, but it describes Earl's business bent. A bit of everything. I remembered that I heard someone mention that Earl was going to be selling cell phones and pagers."

"Really? That's great," she said with obvious relief. "I'll check it out as soon as I can. I thought I was going to have to go back to Seattle to get a replacement."

Doubting it would go over with her, he said, "If he can't help you, maybe you could consider being phone-less while you're here. It could be liberating for you."

She grimaced. "You make it sound as if the phone is a millstone around my neck."

"Isn't it?"

She exhaled. "No, it's a terrific convenience, and a necessary one."

"Sure," he said. No point arguing. "Good luck with your phone hunt." He went around to get in the truck, with a quick glance at Alegra as she strode confidently toward the wraparound porch of the Victorian. He must have imagined any vulnerability in the woman on the ferry. She knew who she was. She was in control. She'd have a phone in an hour, one way or the other, and her world would be right again. Snap. Problem gone. He pulled out of the exit and headed farther north.

Just half a block later, he turned left and slipped into the last parking slot in front of the wood-fronted building that housed the *Beacon*. He'd only been gone since early morning, off to Seattle to look for a new press for the paper, though he'd soon decided against it. He'd let Boyd Posey, his right-hand man who knew the old press inside and out, take over and find its replacement. He didn't want to waste time in Seattle.

As he got out of the truck and took the two steps up to the wooden walkway, then opened the half-glass door to the newspaper office, he thought about his attachment to Shelter Island.

When he'd left after graduation, he hadn't looked back. He hadn't thought he'd ever come back for more than just a yearly visit or so to see his folks. He'd been out to conquer the world, as he'd told Alegra, and he probably had by some people's standards. Not his. His world was here, on the island, with his son and his son's grandparents, a world to be lived in, not conquered.

His parents hadn't asked too many questions when he came back. He was glad. He was home. That was it.

The *Beacon* hadn't changed much since he'd been a kid. The furniture was old, dark and heavy, and the reception desk ran side to side, making a barrier between the entry and the back offices. Stacks of the current issue of the paper sat on the counter, fronted by a brass plaque that held an imprint of their banner—The Beacon, The Island's Voice. Boxes of handouts from local businesses aimed at the tourists here for the festival were placed on the other end. Photos on the walls dated from years ago to the present, and headlines of their biggest stories were highlighted on a special board near the door. He liked the way the place looked, liked its smell of age.

He glanced at the man sitting behind the reception desk, and it was obvious Boyd was so intent on what he was doing on the computer he hadn't heard Joe come in. Sixty years old and bald-headed, Boyd was thin to the point of emaciation, with hawklike features and skin so pale you'd doubt it had ever seen the sun.

"Boyd?" Joe said. Boyd jumped at the sound of his name and closed the lid on the laptop before he turned to look up at Joe, who knew he'd been playing a game. Boyd had been with the *Beacon* for almost thirty years, as much a fixture as anything else in the office, and Joe didn't care what he did on his downtime, as long as he could depend on him to get the paper out.

"I thought you'd be gone more than a day," Boyd said. "Does your quick return mean we have a new press?"

"Nope. It just means I'm back early."

Boyd crossed his arms on his narrow chest and motioned with his head to the back of the space. "I knew they cost an arm and a leg, so I can understand if we have to nurse that beast along awhile more."

"That's not it," Joe said. "I decided that you know a lot more than I do about what we need and so you should be the one to do the buying. Why don't you go over during the festival and see what you can find?"

The man's jaw dropped open. "Me, go and get us a new

press?" He got to his feet, and for the first time in a long time, Joe saw color in his cheeks. "I get to pick it out?"

Joe nodded. "That's about it, within reason."

Boyd's eyes narrowed. "How much are we talking about spending?"

Joe named a figure and Boyd exhaled on a low whistle. "That'll do it. I can get you a terrific press for that."

"Then make it happen."

"Can't say I'll miss the opening ceremonies of the festival. All that damn cannon banging and explosions. Pirates were a noisy lot."

"Bloody, too," Joe murmured, then had a thought. "Do you know if Earl sells cell phones? I heard he did, but…"

"Yeah, that and them expensive white chocolates." He looked quizzically at Joe. "You want a new cell phone?"

"No, a lady on the ferry lost hers and I told her I thought Earl might be able to help her." Joe hesitated, then, "Have you ever heard of Alegra Reynolds?"

"Can't say as I have, Joe. That's the lady?"

"Yeah. She's the founder of the Alegra's Closet boutiques."

That brought an instant smile to Boyd's face. "She's on the island? What's she doing? Going to start one of those stores of hers around these parts?"

"She said she's here for the festival and buying art."

"Shoot, too bad. This place could use a little spicing up. Do you suppose she wears those little nothings that pass for clothes?" He leaned closer. "Is she hot?"

Something in Joe recoiled at the idea of someone talking about Alegra this way, and it didn't help that Boyd's words brought images to his mind that made his body start to tighten. "She's not ugly." A true understatement.

He went around the reception desk and across to his open office door, then entered his cluttered cubicle. He took his seat behind a desk almost hidden by stacks of paperwork. His old swivel chair protested when he turned in it toward the computer on the left. He booted the thing up and went straight to the Internet. He typed in *Alegra Reynolds,* then hit the enter key.

ALEGRA GOT TO Earl Money's store just as he was closing, and thankfully, he'd been more than happy to stay open a bit longer to set her up with a cell phone that turned out to be an upgrade from her old unit. By the time she got back to her cottage at Snug Harbor, it was past dinner and she decided to just eat one of the energy bars she brought. She used the Internet access in her room, got in touch with Roz, and in a few hours, had all of the data from her old phone downloaded into her new one.

After that, she worked on her laptop, going over reports until just around midnight. When she was about to close down the computer, she reconsidered. She went to a search engine and put in the name of the high school on the island. She was a bit surprised to find that the Grace High School had its own Web page. Nothing fancy, just a picture of the school as it was when it started fifty years ago and one of how it looked now.

She saw the links on the left, tapped on the alumni link and entered the year she graduated. The screen flashed with an image of the yearbook, and she entered her old name, Peterson. Suddenly, there she was ten years ago, a head-and-shoulders shot of her with long, pale hair pulled back from her face with a headband. Anyone would have called her expression sober, but they'd have been wrong. It was desperation, the same desperation that drove her to leave a week later.

Under the photo with her name was the heading Predictions For Al's Future, followed by a blank space, because she'd never given the editor anything to put there.

She clicked on an earlier year, then another, and on her third try, she found Joe Lawrence.

The man as a boy looked so young and thin, with a shock of dark hair falling over a smooth, earnest face. He was smiling, and it was the same boyish smile she'd seen on the ferry, though his adult face had a decided sexiness his young face hadn't. She didn't really remember him from the past, except once, at the lighthouse, she'd gone there to hide out and three boys had been there before her. She glared at them until they'd gone.

She glanced at the predictions for his future: Pulitzer Prize winner by 30, a millionaire by 40, living in the south of France forever. He'd known what he wanted and hadn't been afraid to see it in print. But as far as she knew there'd been no Pulitzer Prize, no millions—look at the old truck he drove—and Shelter Island was a long way from the south of France.

She closed her computer, then sat back in the chair and sighed. So much for a trip down memory lane.

She stood and crossed to the dresser to get ready for bed. In half an hour she was in the comfortable canopy bed, staring up at the shadows. Her yearbook picture flitted through her mind, then was replaced by Joe's. As sleep tugged at her, the face changed to the man of the present....

Chapter Three

The dream was simple, nothing convoluted or strange, the way some of Alegra's dreams could be. It was just Joe on the ferry watching her as she held her phone. He was coming closer, touching her hand with his, taking the phone, then saying she had to let it go and tossing it over the railing. In the dream she heard the splash when it hit the water, not like the reality that had played out hours earlier.

The dream started to repeat, and this time when he reached for the phone, she refused to give it to him. He shook his head, those blue eyes almost sad. She didn't want his pity. He reached out again, but not for the phone. For *her.* Then she was in his arms, and his heat was everywhere....

Alegra woke to a room of hazy shadows and rolled onto her side. She was surprised that the illuminated hands of the clock showed nine-fifteen. Her "late" mornings normally were when she slept until seven instead of six. And she hardly ever remembered her dreams. But when she shifted onto her back and closed her eyes, the dream from last night was there. Joe grabbing her phone and tossing it, then her being pulled into his arms. Both dreams left her feeling oddly unsettled.

With a deep sigh, she pushed herself up. She couldn't see any sign of sunlight in the long sliver of space between the drapes. Typical island weather—foggy. She headed to the bathroom, with its clawfoot tub and shower stall. She stayed under the hot stream of water for a long time before she got out and dressed simply in a long white shirt and charcoal-gray corduroy slacks. She combed her hair straight back off of her face and into a simple ponytail, and hesitated as she caught her image in the mirror over the pedestal sink.

She thought of her old yearbook picture. There was no desperation in her eyes now, just determination.

After logging on to her laptop and finding a slew of e-mails—mostly about a faulty supplier for the Houston stores—she got down to work trying to figure out what to do. By the time she had the problem settled, it was almost noon. She'd meant it when she said she planned to do some art shopping. A business associate had told her about Angelo's gallery, said it had the best work on the island. Well, now was as good a time as any.

She tucked in her shirt, slipped on her brown leather bomber jacket, then grabbed her car keys, her wallet and new cell phone. She pushed them into her pockets, left the cottage and stopped on the veranda to glance at the view from the bluffs. If it had been clear, the view would be stunning, but right now it was blocked by the remnants of the fog that hung over the dark waters far below.

She went down the steps onto the crushed shell walkway that led toward the main house and parking lot. Despite the drab day, the old Victorian looked lovely, all cream and forest-green, with elaborate gingerbread trim on its multiple spires and in the corners of the supports for the wraparound porch. She got to her car, hit the remote and as the car locks clicked open, someone called out to her in an almost painfully cheery voice. "Ms. Reynolds!"

She turned to see at the side entry of the house a young woman of maybe eighteen, dressed in a ridiculously frilly apron over plain old jeans and a blue shirt. Martha, Melanie? Alegra couldn't remember how the girl had introduced herself when she'd checked in yesterday. "Good morning," she called back, keeping the car door open.

"I was just wondering if we can plan on you joining us for tea at four o'clock."

An English tea in the main house with the other guests balancing fine china and conversation didn't appeal to her at all. "No, I don't think so."

"How about dinner?"

She had to eat. "Okay, but I'll take it in my cottage."

"Just let us know what time, then." The girl sounded disappointed. "Have a lovely day."

The girl would have gone back inside if Alegra hadn't called out to her. "Can you tell me where Angelo's art gallery is?"

"Sure." She motioned to the exit of the parking area. "Turn right, go down about a block or so, and it's on the other side of the street. It's the only two-story building on that block. There're a couple more galleries a ways past it, The Place and Jenny's Treasures. Also, they'll be setting up an art show near the gazebo in the park next door."

"Thanks," Alegra called back, and with a wave climbed in her car. She drove out onto the main street, but didn't follow the girl's directions. She knew where Angelo's was as soon as the girl had said it was a two-story building. But she also knew that she was procrastinating. She had more important things to do on the island. Important, but difficult. She'd find the gallery after she was finished.

She turned back toward the way she'd come from the ferry, then about halfway to the dock, she turned onto a road that went into the heart of the island. She hadn't been on this road for ten years, but the deep gloom that shrouded it was very familiar.

She passed a scattering of orchards and old bungalows, then spotted her turn. She slowed to a crawl and for a moment thought of just turning around and going back to the gallery to look at paintings and do this later. But instead, she braced herself and turned onto a narrow lane choked by trees and overgrown brush trees.

She went up a small hill and knew the exact moment when she crossed the boundary into the land where she'd been born and lived for eighteen years. She saw the house right away, despite the untended vegetation that pressed all around it. The faded blue walls were chalky and weather-stained. The windows were blank, but unbroken, and the porch sagged precariously.

She pulled the car to a stop and just sat there staring at the house. Why had she dreaded this so much? There was no repeat of the ridiculous tears from the day before. This place meant nothing to her. It was just an old, neglected place that, now that she'd seen it, she could mark off her list and put up for sale, as she should have done years ago, after her father had died. She'd forget about it the way she would this island, forever. She pulled away and didn't look back, just the way she hadn't looked back when she'd walked away from the house after graduation with eleven dollars in her pocket.

By the time she drove back into town, her mind was on art. She'd taken up collecting a few years ago when she'd spotted a canvas in an art gallery in New York. It was just a simple work by an unknown artist, depicting a road that wound through a rocky countryside, going off into a horizon splashed with the rich colors of sunset. It drew her in, and she'd bought it on impulse.

Since then, she'd picked up a few paintings here and there with similar themes, roads or paths heading into the distance to an unknown goal. She never analyzed why she felt a connection to those scenes, but in every city she visited, she sought out more of the same. Sometimes she found something, most times she didn't. But she was going to do the same thing on the island. It would be one spot of pleasure in this ordeal.

She drove slowly along the main street, which was a

lot busier than the day before. She passed the Snug Harbor B&B and spotted Angelo's gallery on the other side of the street another block down. She pulled into what appeared to be the only available parking spot and climbed out of the car.

Her cell phone rang. She dug it out of her pocket and flipped it open. "Hey, Roz, what's going on?"

She turned to head up the two steps to the wooden walkway. Just as Roz started to tell her about a distribution meeting that had been called for the next day, someone ran into her left side. She would have gone right off the edge of the walkway if a hand hadn't grabbed her by her upper arm.

A voice was saying, "Oh, man, I'm sorry, I didn't see you there." The voice was familiar. As familiar as the deep blue eyes she met when she turned toward the voice. Joe.

Seeing him right by her, holding her, startled her as much as the collision moments earlier had, and she found herself acting without thinking, jerking back and free of his touch. "You almost knocked me into next week!" she said.

Joe let her go, but didn't move back. Instead, he hunkered down, then quickly straightened up. He had her phone, was offering it to her. She stared at it, knowing she must have dropped it when they collided, then she heard Roz yelling through the earpiece, "Alegra? Alegra! What's going on?"

She took it quickly from Joe and pressed it against her ear. "Roz, I'm sorry, I dropped the phone. I'll have to call you back." She flipped it shut, then turned the phone over in her hand. It had a scuff mark, but other than that, looked okay.

"You didn't kill it," Joe said.

"That's all I'd need." She pushed it into her jacket pocket. "It took me ages to download all my information into it."

His eyes flicked over her, then back to her face. "I bet it did."

Was that sarcasm? She felt a touch of heat in her face. "I'm fully connected now."

That brought a crooked smile to his lips. "I take it that's a good thing?"

It occurred to her that he, for some reason, had come back here whipped and beaten, and because of that, resented anyone he saw as successful. The man was handsome and sexy, but he was an islander and obviously a loser. It was a combination that should have killed any attraction she felt for him. But it didn't. "Whatever."

He frowned. "You know, that's truly annoying."

"Excuse me?" She frowned right back at him.

"The word *whatever.* It's annoying. It shows indifference to something, maybe even scorn. It's a lousy word that gets used far too much. People should just say, 'I don't give a damn.'"

The heat in her face now wasn't entirely a product of being irritated by his penchant for defining words, good or bad. It was because she was anything but indifferent to this man. Instead of arguing, she said with exaggerated pronunciation, "Whatever."

To her surprise he chuckled roughly and held his hands up, palms out. "Okay, okay, I give up."

"Good decision," she said.

He cocked his head to one side and considered her for a long moment. "Were you coming here to see me and give me a good human-interest piece for the paper? I can see it now. 'Alegra Reynolds of Alegra's Closet fame, visits our island for—'?"

She cut that off with a fast, "No," as she realized she'd parked right in front of the *Beacon.* He must have been coming out of his office. But as the single word hung between them, she had second thoughts. She'd planned to avoid all the islanders until the time was right to tell everyone who she'd been and who she was now; she hadn't wanted anyone to stumble over her past identity until she was ready. But maybe there was a better way.

Joe, no matter what he'd been in the past, ran the only newspaper in town. What if she let him see Alegra Reynolds, what she accomplished, where she was going, the things that would provide background to the story that would surely be front page news? For when she went to the ball on the last night of the festival, when she finally stood up in front of the islanders and handed them a check to go into a fund for town improvements, an amount that would stun most of the people there, it would be a big story. Meanwhile, it wouldn't be a bad idea for one person to know what she'd accomplished in the years since she'd left the island.

He'd seen her hesitation and continued, "Nothing too intrusive. Just a 'Guess who's at the festival' sort of story."

"Sure, why not?" she asked.

"Great. If you have time later on, maybe we can—"

"I was on my way to Angelo's art gallery. I had to park here—it's packed by the gallery."

"Parking's pretty tight with the festival starting tomorrow. That's why Angelo has a parking area behind his building."

"Good to know for future reference," she said, and had an idea how to start passing information to Joe. "Since you're a local, is there any secret about approaching Angelo if I want to buy something?"

"You mean, to get a deal?" he asked with a crooked smile.

She nodded. "It never hurts to save money."

"One thing to keep in mind is, Angelo Paloma is very protective of the artists he shows. He likes haggling and selling the product. The only suggestion I'd have is, don't accept the first price he gives you."

"Thanks. I'll keep that in mind."

He nodded. "I've got a bit of time on my hands at the moment. Why don't I go with you and introduce you to Angelo and we can get started on the story?"

If she'd learned one thing in business it was that if you wanted something, you never acted too eager, whether it was buying a painting or getting your facts to the right person. "I don't want to take you away from big stories you have to cover."

"That's a joke, isn't it?"

"You said you run this newspaper, and there have to be stories that need your attention."

"Not at the moment, at least, not beyond the preparation for the festival. A good story about Alegra Reynolds visiting the island, maybe thinking of expanding here, now that's important."

He was so far off the mark for why she was here that it wasn't even funny. "That isn't going to happen." Opening a store of hers in this place was as unlikely as a five-headed alien kidnapping the mayor of the town. "This island isn't ready for an Alegra's Closet."

"How do you know that?" he drawled. "We're more progressive than you might think."

"No hammer and chisel, not anymore, from what I've heard."

"See? Exactly my point. We grow with the times, and if that growth means an Alegra's Closet right here on the main street, well, so be it."

"Hey, boss," a voice said as the door to the offices of the newspaper opened.

Alegra looked past Joe at another man, and while she hadn't seen him since he'd been at their house drinking with her father, she recognized Boyd Posey right away. He'd been skinny, pinched and balding back then, and now he was skinny, pinched and completely bald. He'd worked at the *Beacon* all those years ago, and he obviously was still working there.

Joe turned to him, but the man was looking past his boss at Alegra. His eyes narrowed and for a second she was certain he remembered her as well as she remembered him. But she knew how misplaced that paranoia was when he spoke again. "Oh, sorry, Joe. I didn't see you were talking to a beautiful woman." He never looked away from Alegra when he went on, this time talking to her. "Ma'am, I'm Boyd Posey, assistant editor at the *Beacon.*"

"I'm Alegra Reynolds."

His mouth formed a silent *O.* She had seen the reaction many times before. Recognition—but not because he recognized her as Al Peterson, but rather, he knew her as the woman whose "empire was built on lace and underwiring," as a gentleman with the same expression had once told her. "Alegra Reynolds of Alegra's Closet fame? Well, isn't that something," he drawled with a slightly lascivious glint in his pale eyes. "My wife's got your catalogs." He laughed. "Not that she can wear the stuff, but she can dream."

Joe cut in. "What was it you needed, Boyd?"

Boyd let his gaze linger on Alegra for a long moment before he turned back to Joe. "You didn't say if you're coming back."

"I don't know. I'll check in later."

Boyd met Alegra's eyes again. "Do you model your clothes?"

She didn't remember liking or disliking Boyd in the past. He'd been a drinking buddy of her father's and he hardly even noticed her. But now she was edging toward not liking him. Forcing a "business as usual" expression that she had mastered over the years, she shook her head. "I just design and sell my stock."

"Too bad," Boyd murmured, then went back inside.

She felt Joe by her side, and heard him say on a sigh, "Should I apologize for Boyd?"

"Don't bother. It goes with the territory," she said, looking down the street to the building she knew housed the gallery. "Everyone has a reaction to what I do, and sometimes it's less than complimentary."

"Believe it or not, Boyd *was* complimenting you."

"Whatever," she said as she turned back to him.

He smiled at that. "A good use of that word for a change."

That was when he touched her arm. "Come on. Angelo is waiting to dazzle you with his inventory of brilliant art."

She wanted Joe to go with her, but that didn't mean she wanted contact with him. She moved away from his touch as she took off toward the gallery. He fell into step beside her.

The bottom level of the gallery was framed by brick and the upper level by silvered wood siding. The roof showed spots of green moss, and it was pitched high in the middle over the entry.

The building had been a feed store when she'd lived here, with rough wooden floors and huge beams overhead that had held winches to lift hay bales in and out of the lofts. The place looked very much as it had back then, except there were deep windows now where the loading doors had once been, and a new entrance had been fashioned between them with carved double doors. Joe took a step ahead of her, grasped the heavy-hasp latch and pushed the door back for her.

"For what it's worth," he said, "I can promise you that Angelo won't give you any grief over your choice of careers."

She stepped inside. Glancing around, she saw that all remnants of the feed store were gone, except for what was retained for decorative impact. The subtle scent of woodsy incense hung in the air. The space still soared through both stories, but now it was a grand area to display paintings and sculpture. The floors were highly polished hardwood, and stairs, fashioned of wood and iron, swept up in the middle to a second display space upstairs. Soft harp music drifted around them, and the peace in the place was palpable.

A disembodied voice with a very British clip to it cut through that softness, coming from somewhere near the rear of the building. "Greetings! Please, help yourself to tea or coffee from the table by the windows, and I'll be right there."

"Angelo? It's me, Joe," Joe called.

"I'm talking to London. Give me a minute."

"You got it." Joe motioned to an oval table that held tea things, along with some shortbread cookies. "Like anything?" he asked.

"Oh, no, thanks," she said, and looked at the nearest grouping of paintings.

"Then why don't we just browse until Angelo's free. Anything in particular that might strike your fancy?"

She couldn't explain to him what she was looking for, because she didn't know until she saw it. "I'll just look around," she said.

"I'll tag along, if you don't mind, and you can tell me about the art you already have."

What would she tell him? *I collect roads that go nowhere?* She didn't think so, but she spoke softly, "Okay," and went into a large alcove formed by three floating walls butted up against each other in the shape of a *U.* When she saw an elegantly simple gold plaque on a slim stand by the three prints, she stopped and stared at it.

Works by Sean Payne—Local Artist.

Her past hit her with such force the room started to swim. She took a deep breath, and the room settled, but the pain in her middle didn't ease. Sean, skinny and mean and taunting her. She had to struggle not to rush out of the gallery.

Chapter Four

Alegra was aware of Joe looking at her, and she was certain he'd ask what was going on. But he surprised her. When she stopped in front of the two paintings of Sean's on display, he simply stood by her side silently. Any paintings Sean had created as a kid had come from a spray can and been done on some poor sucker's blank wall. Now it was oil paints on stretched canvases, rendered in almost angry strokes.

She studied the first one, a three-foot-by-four-foot, unframed canvas labeled *Celebration*. It was a scene depicting Bartholomew Grace's celebration, pirates and wenches partying in a lavish room. On a balcony high above the revelers was a lone figure. He was more shadow than light, the suggestion of a billowing shirt and snug breeches. A mug was held high in one hand, and what looked like a bloody dagger in the other.

"Bartholomew Grace," Joe said in a low voice. "The king of debauchery immortalized in art."

She started to say something, but stopped when she

saw the next painting—Light of Home. A simple rendering, it depicted the old lighthouse on the northern tip of the island, what she'd always thought of as *her* lighthouse. The place she went to dream of a future away from the island, imagining the beacon showing the way. The painting showed the lighthouse as it once functioned, its beacon penetrating the incoming fog.

She took in the rugged promontory that soared over the beach below it, rendered in quick, harsh strokes of the artist's brush. Although details were few, Sean had caught the heart of the old place as it looked in those fleeting moments between day and night, when the fog crept in, and the light was fading. Massive waves crashed at the base of the cliffs, up and over the huge rock at the base where she'd spent so much time as a child.

Why should a painting that showed the only sanctuary she'd had as a child have been created by one of her tormenters?

"That's the original lighthouse on the island, on the northern end," Joe was saying. "It's a favorite of artists and photographers."

"It's very…interesting," she said unevenly.

"The artist grew up on the island."

"He still lives here?" she asked, never taking her eyes off of the painting.

"No, he mostly lives in San Francisco, but he comes back now and then."

Sean lived in the same city where she lived part of the year. Millions of people lived there, but still it was unsettling to think she could have rounded a corner and run into Sean Payne with no warning.

"Sean's had a hard time in his life, personal problems mostly, bad choices," Joe was saying. "But his art seems to get better and better. Maybe it's that old saying about suffering bringing out genius."

Alegra heard his words, waiting for some sense of satisfaction to hit her that Sean hadn't had it easy, that the misery he'd once put her through had been repaid. But it didn't come.

"Ah, Joseph." The same voice that had greeted them when they came in sounded behind them.

Alegra turned to see a man who was almost as wide as he was tall, his bald pate ringed by dark hair long enough to be pulled back from his florid face in a ponytail. He was dressed all in black and wore what appeared to be sheepskin slippers on his feet. He was smiling, a toothy expression, and half glasses were tipped low on his nose so pale eyes could peer over them.

"Angelo," Joe said, reaching out a hand to shake the gallery owner's. "I want to introduce you to Alegra Reynolds. She's been enjoying Sean's paintings."

Angelo turned to Alegra with obvious pleasure. "Well, so, you appreciate our Sean, do you?"

She wouldn't go that far, but motioned to the light-house painting and surprised herself by asking, "How much is it?"

He clasped his pudgy hands together over his ample stomach and didn't even glance at the piece before he gave her a figure she was quite sure had been inflated as far as it could go without exploding. "He's well worth it," he added as he moved closer to it and pushed his glasses up to peer at the painting through the lenses. "I have never decided if that's a ship in the fog or just a curl of the mists."

Alegra couldn't see what he was talking about, and didn't care. She took out her wallet and handed him her credit card. "I'll take it."

Angelo looked taken aback. "That's great," he said, taking the card, then waving it between them. "I shall return in a moment." He headed off toward the back of the building.

Joe looked at her. "I don't think you understood. You should have countered with a lower price. I'm sure he would have come down."

She didn't care. The money was nothing to her. She wasn't even sure why she'd bought it at all, except she'd considered going to the lighthouse to take a picture of it. Now she didn't have to. She'd take it back to either her New York apartment or her town house in San Francisco. She might hang it or she might not. She'd just take it with her, and the last thing she'd wanted was to haggle over the price.

"It doesn't matter," she said.

Angelo came back then, got her signature and promised to have the painting delivered to the Snug Harbor B&B later that day. "It's a wonderful painting," he said. "Sean is so talented, and so tortured."

All Alegra wanted to do now was leave, so she thanked him and headed for the door. When she stepped out into the growing cold and failing light, Joe was right behind her. She didn't have to look to know that, she could feel him close to her. Then he was at her side, falling into step with her. "Remind me to sell you some land in the Everglades."

"I don't buy swamp land," she murmured on her way to the car.

"But you buy overpriced paintings?"

She bit back a *whatever* and said simply, "It seems so." She unlocked the door, then grabbed the handle and turned to Joe. "It made Angelo happy."

"And it made *you* happy," Joe said.

No, it hadn't. But it did make her feel as if something in her was completed. "I've got my painting, and Angelo can buy more tea and pastries."

"And Sean has one of the biggest sales in his career."

"Really?"

"As far as I can tell, he's made some sales here and there, but nothing that's made him a major name. Maybe if people know that he's being collected by someone like you, they'll take another look at his work."

"I doubt that," she said. "I think Angelo spotlighting him at the gallery gives him more prestige. A man with great taste believes in him."

That made Joe laugh. "The reason I told you that Angelo wouldn't give you any grief over your business if he knew who you were was because he wasn't always Angelo Paloma, art dealer extraordinaire. He was Andy Peal in another life."

She knew the name immediately. "You're kidding!"

She knew it had been a while, but at one time Andy Peal had produced several over-the-top off-Broadway shows. In fact, she'd used a theme from one of his shows in a photo shoot for one of her first spring lines. "It's a small world," she murmured at the same time her cell rang.

"Go ahead and answer it," Joe said, as if giving her permission to do what she would have done anyway. "And enjoy your painting. I'll be in touch about the story for the *Beacon*." With that he disappeared into his office.

Her caller was Roz, who proceeded to give her the details of a robbery in one of their new stores in St. Louis. Alegra just sat there in the car and listened. "You won't believe what they stole," Roz said. "All of our sequined and bejeweled bras, every last one."

The bras bordered on being tacky, but they were big sellers. "I'm sure they'll show up online any time now," Alegra said.

Roz told her she was contacting the insurance company. "I thought it was sort of weird, though. No perfume, no panties, not even that new scented-oil line. Just the bras."

"Let me know what the insurance company says," Alegra said, then hung up and sank back in the seat with the phone resting on her thigh. At last she started the car and pulled out onto the street. She turned north, away from her cottage at Snug Harbor. She knew where she was going before the idea was fully formed. She was going to see the lighthouse.

WHEN JOE DID a name search on Alegra to get more background on her before starting his story, he could find no pictures of her and little information about her personal life, beyond that she was twenty-eight, both parents deceased—she was raised by her grandmother—and had homes in New York and San Francisco; one article mentioned that she'd graduated from a small city college with a degree in design. There were a lot of articles about her business, even one in *Who's Who in Business*.

One thing seemed clear—Alegra was a driven woman who lived for her work and buried herself in the business. He'd known women like that before, had even married one—Jean, for whom work had been everything. But he couldn't criticize her. Back then, work had been all-consuming for him, too.

They hadn't been married six months when they both realized that marriage wasn't for them. But before they could remedy it, Jean discovered she was pregnant. They had decided to stay married until the baby came, see if things changed. See if they could make it work. But alas, they couldn't. His focus didn't shift. Neither did hers. And so the marriage was over. Alex stayed with him and a string of nannies and Jean left.

When Joe left the office, around six, he climbed into his truck and headed north of town to the house where he'd grown up and the place he'd returned to when he'd come back to live on the island. Ten minutes later, he pulled into the driveway of the sprawling ranch-style bungalow perched on the bluffs and parked beside his father's new car.

He took the steps to the wraparound veranda two at

a time, went into the house and called out to his mother. Silence. Then he saw a note taped to the mirror of an umbrella stand near the front entry. *Took Alex into town to watch them set up for the festival. Back by seven.* He found a pen, wrote, *Out walking,* on the bottom of the note, then left by the back door.

He crossed the twenty-foot stretch of grass that separated the house from the top of the bluffs, went down the wooden steps his dad had built for beach access years ago and jumped the last two steps to land with both feet on the sand. He barely glanced at the choppy water before he set off. He knew where he was going, and finally saw the lighthouse high on the bluff rising into the darkening skies.

The structure looked strong and solid, despite its surface being faded and weathered. The glass at the top that protected the lights—the beam had been turned off years ago—looked as gray as the sky. He'd brought Alex here within days of returning to the island. It had given him a deep sense of continuity in this life. His father had played here as a child. He himself played here, and then he'd watched his son play on the rocks and sand. Peace about his decision to come home had settled on him right then, and he knew he'd done the right thing.

He trudged along, keeping clear of the surf, and finally reached an outcropping at the bottom of the cliffs that was the foundation for the soaring section of rock that supported the lighthouse—and then realized he wasn't the only one who'd come here today. Sitting on a huge rock, her arms wrapped around bent knees, her head resting on those knees, was Alegra. Every nerve in his body hummed to life.

Joe watched her for a full minute, wondering about his reaction to seeing her here. In some inexplicable way, she'd gotten under his skin. A mainlander, a woman who'd be here only briefly. His feelings made no sense at all, and he shook them off.

He started for the rock, his feet silent on the packed sand. He saw Alegra slowly lift her head, raising her face into the growing breeze. Her chin was up, her eyes closed, and he was struck by how very beautiful she was. He reached the side of the huge rock before he called out a hello.

She turned quickly at the sound of his voice, and saw him. There was no smile in greeting, just those amber eyes wide. "I'm sorry," he said quickly. "I didn't mean to intrude."

Without a word, she slid off the other side of the rock to the sand. He made his way around until he was near her, and watched her brushing any clinging grains of sand off her slacks. Then her actions stilled, and he saw her flex her fingers before she took an audible breath. "I came to see the lighthouse," she said in an oddly flat voice, staring past him to the sound.

"So, what do you think of it?" he asked.

"It's incredible," she said. "It looks as if it's going to be foggy tonight."

"Fog is a staple around here," he said, wishing she'd look at him.

She closed her eyes for a moment, then at last turned her gaze on him, but her long lashes shadowed the expression in her eyes. "Why isn't the lighthouse beacon on?"

"It hasn't been lit for years. It's in bad shape, and the historical society keeps talking about restoring it or tearing it down. But they never seem to get around to raising the money to do either."

"How much would be needed to restore it?"

He named a figure that had been bandied around.

"Well, it'd be a shame if it was torn down," she said as she dropped to a crouch and picked up a handful of damp sand. She closed her hand tightly on the sand. When she opened her fingers, the sand was compressed into a tight ball, the dampness binding it together firmly. "Crazy sand," she murmured. "I remember making a castle when I was young, just sand and water and an old drinking cup to fashion the turrets. It would have lasted forever if the waves hadn't come in and destroyed it."

"Where did you grow up?" he couldn't help asking.

She let the ball of sand roll off her hand to hit the beach and refragment. Then she stood, dusted her hands and said vaguely, without making eye contact, "Near the water." She moved past him toward the shore.

He followed. "Which water? Lakes, streams or oceans?"

"The Pacific and then the Atlantic."

This was like pulling teeth. "Any particular city on the ocean?"

"None you'd have heard of," she said.

He copied her stare out over the sound to the city on

the far shore, and decided to let it go for now. "We built castles," he found himself saying. "And pirate forts some of the time, but no matter what we did to protect them, the tide came in and they'd be gone the next time we came down. We'd remake them. I can't count how many times we did that, over and over again." He chuckled softly. "The optimism of youth. Always believing that the next time would be the charm. Live and learn."

"Kids always have hope, even when adults see things as set and hopeless," she said softly.

He turned to look at her. He was talking about water and sand, but he sensed she was not. Her jaw looked set, and he saw her hand clenched at her side. He wished he understood what had been said to bring that tension on, but knew better than to ask. All he'd get was another maddeningly vague answer that would only leave him with more questions. So he asked something simple.

"Are you hungry?"

She blinked, then hugged her arms around herself before she looked up at him. "Yes, as a matter of fact, I am."

He would love to see that tension leave her and a smile come to her lips. So he plowed on with an invitation that he didn't even think about before offering it. "I'm hungry, too, so how about coming with me to get something to eat? We can talk about the article for the *Beacon*."

He didn't let himself think about why he shouldn't be asking this woman to have dinner with him and why he *should* be asking her to come to the office for an interview. If he were honest, he knew he wanted more than dinner with her. That was the truly foolish part. She was everything he didn't need in a woman. A woman married to her job.

But maybe that was it. She was a mainlander who would go back to the mainland to carry on her business, and he'd do a story about her presence on the island. So she'd leave, and he'd still be here. It was that simple. He could spend some time in the company of a beautiful, intriguing woman, build a story, then that would be that.

Her cell phone rang. She took it from the pocket of her soft leather jacket and answered it. "Roz?"

As she listened, she stared down at the sand under her feet. "Sorry, I don't know off the top of my head." She shifted from foot to foot on the sand. "I know, I know, and I will. I'll get the figures to you as soon as I can. Give me a couple of hours." She closed the phone.

"Business calling again?"

"Business always calls, but I do have to eat," she said. "Maybe there's a fast-food place around where we can talk?"

"No fast food, but some good restaurants. How did you get here?"

"I drove and parked up there." She pointed to the top of the bluffs to the south of where they stood. "There's a clearing off the road and some steps down. You know where that is?"

Islanders knew about that spot, but if he was thinking of the right one, you couldn't see it from the road. It was halfway between where they were and his house. He wondered how she'd found it, but he simply said, "Yeah, I do."

"How did *you* get here?" she asked.

"I walked down the beach from my house."

"Then why don't we take my car?" she said.

He agreed and they began walking.

They were at the steps cut into the bluffs that would take them to the clearing above when her phone rang again. They both stopped.

"It'll just take a minute," she said.

She spoke to the same person again—Roz—and whatever was being said on the other end made Alegra frown deeply. Damn it, he wished she'd smile, but it seemed answering the phone usually made her frown. He watched her start to nibble on her bottom lip. "I know, I know, but…" She turned a little away from him as if for privacy. "Deal with the insurance, and tell Hank to cooperate any way he can." A pause. "Of course, I understand. I'll call you back as soon as I can."

Joe watched her and took a step back. He didn't want to eat between phone calls, and doing any sort of interview wouldn't work with that kind of interruption. Maybe this was the time to walk away and regroup. He said, "We'll do this later," to Alegra's back, and started off along the beach. He'd gone about fifty yards when he heard her call, "Joe, where are you going?"

He turned around to look at her, but kept walking backward as he shouted, "Take care of business, and we'll meet up later for the interview."

"I can do two things at the same time!" she insisted.

He turned and didn't slow his pace. "Whatever," he called over his shoulder, and kept going, building distance between himself and Alegra and knowing his actions bordered on childish. But he needed to get back to his own life, forget what he'd been thinking at the lighthouse. He'd do the article, and keep his relationship with Alegra on that ground.

He didn't look back.

Chapter Five

Alegra was ready to hurry after Joe until he called out, "Whatever," without even breaking stride. She started up the steps. "It was a phone call, for Pete's sake, a frigging phone call," she grumbled. "It was business!" she shouted to the empty air around her as she stepped into the clearing and headed for her car.

Fury was growing inside her. It was just a phone call, and he'd walked away like a kid who didn't like the rules of the game and was going to take his ball and go home. Well, she'd find food for herself, and let him come to her if he really wanted to do the piece for the newspaper.

She put the car in gear and headed back toward town. Her plans didn't depend on the damn interview. That was just icing on the cake for her. As she drove back to town, her anger began to fade.

If she were honest with herself, she'd sort of looked forward to having a meal with him, and talking and trying to figure the man out. But the fact was, he was an islander, and nothing outside of the island counted for anything to him. Just as well he'd walked away. Spending time with him would have been counterproductive. She certainly wasn't looking for anything from him, beyond making sure he got a good slant on her before the last night of the festival. She certainly wasn't looking for any sort of relationship. Not even a brief one.

Oddly though, without the anger, she was left with a sense of flatness, of disappointment. She remembered that feeling as a child when she thought something good might happen, then finding out that nothing good was *ever* going to happen.

She slowed on the main street, which now was alive with activity. More streamers were being put up, and when she neared the Snug Harbor, she saw that the park by it was almost filled with booths, all displaying Jolly Roger flags. The statue of Bartholomew Grace at the entrance looked right at home.

She drove past the bed-and-breakfast, found a small coffee shop where she bought a cup of coffee and a large muffin to take out, then went back to the Snug Harbor and her cottage. Within ten minutes she was at her computer, nibbling on the muffin and sipping the coffee. She sent the information Roz needed to deal with the police, then answered the e-mails that had built up while she'd been out.

She was vaguely aware of distant voices and noises coming from the nearby park, and every once in a while, a burst of raucous laughter punctuated the other sounds. The girl from the main house called to ask about the dinner she'd said she wanted, and Alegra decided to pass on it. The muffin and coffee would tide her over. She went back to work, made decisions, took care of problems, and when she finally sat back with a deep, tired sigh, she was shocked to see that the room was dark, except for the lights that had come on automatically by the entry and the glow from the computer monitor.

A glance at the clock and she saw it was nearly eight—and she was starving. Her coffee and muffin were long gone. She regretted canceling dinner, and knew it was probably too late to reorder it. Besides, she needed to stretch her legs. She shrugged on her leather jacket, gathered up her wallet, keys and cell phone and left the cottage. The fog had arrived full force, wrapping around the land, blotting out lights and making blurred silhouettes of the other cottages and the main house. It even seemed to muffle the sounds still coming from the park. She heard music start, something that sounded like flutes, mingled with bursts of laughter.

She decided against driving, the fog was so heavy. So she walked out onto the street to find a restaurant. She didn't know what was available now. In her childhood there'd been a choice of only two eateries—a breakfast place and a coffee shop. But with the influx of tourists, surely more had opened.

She set out, passing the park. The music came from speakers set up by the massive gazebo. Men hustled around, putting up tentlike structures over the main area of booths, obviously taking precautions in case it rained.

As she continued on her way down the main street,

she spotted a red neon sign that read Bartholomew's. It hung over the entry to a place that had been styled to look like a pirate ship, complete with a gangplank entry. A wooden sign by the street promised An Adventure In Dining, followed by The Best Beef Around. That got her attention.

She walked up the gangplank, pushed back the door and stepped inside. The pirate ship theme was everywhere, the ever present Jolly Roger draped over a painting of Bartholomew. A man in full pirate garb, right down to the eye patch, was there to greet her.

"Ahoy, there," he said loudly. "How many be there?"

"One be here," Alegra said.

He grinned at her with a mock bow. "Ye got it," he said, then reached for a huge leather-bound menu off a stand by the door.

He led the way through an arched entry into a room that looked like the bowels of a galleon. Dark wood walls, brass fixtures, heavy iron lamps and fake portals on the back wall added to the illusion. The booth he took her to was near the back, a bit too close to what looked like the kitchen entry, and so dark she doubted she'd be able to see her food. But she was too hungry to care at the moment.

She passed on an offered "grog of hot rum," and instead ordered gin and tonic on the rocks. She'd barely settled in the seat and opened the menu before a waitress dressed like a pirate's wench came to the table with her drink and said she'd be back in a bit to get her dinner order.

Alegra took a grateful sip of her drink, then rested

her head against the high back of the booth and closed her eyes. She took several deep breaths and slowly let them out, willing her muscles to relax.

"Having a nap?"

Her eyes flew open at the sound of the familiar male voice. Joe was standing over her, but he'd changed out of his "island traditional" into a white, open-necked shirt worn under a black leather jacket, and with dark pants that clearly defined strong thighs. His hair was combed straight back from his face, and he had obviously just shaved. Damn it, he looked good, and for some reason, that annoyed her.

"Do you ever *not* sneak up on people?" she asked.

"Sorry," he murmured.

Not entirely over his abrupt leave-taking today on the beach, she said rudely, "What do you want?"

He simply glanced at the empty side of the booth and asked, "Are you meeting someone?"

She shook her head, then took another sip of her drink.

"No business meeting?"

She looked at him, then quite deliberately took her phone out of her jacket pocket and laid it on the tablecloth. "Not right now, but who knows?" she said. "The night's young."

"Always ready," he said pleasantly. And that annoyed her even more.

"In business you have to be," she said, the words sounding stuffy even to her. "How about you?" She glanced past him, then met his blue eyes again. "Alone or with company?"

"I thought I had company," he said. "But I was stood up."

She gave in to sarcasm. "She sounds like a smart lady."

Nothing seemed to get to him. "Oh, he's no lady, he's three years old and was here for hours with his grandparents watching them set up for the festival and playing with the other kids. By the time I found them, they were heading home to bed. Since I was still hungry, I came in alone to get something."

She couldn't resist saying, "You could have eaten earlier."

"So could have you," he countered. Again he glanced at her largely empty booth. "How about consolidating our booths? Maybe we can talk before your phone starts ringing."

"Whatever," she said deliberately.

He slipped into the booth, then the waitress was there, handing Joe a menu and asking if he'd like a drink. He ordered a whiskey on the rocks.

When the waitress moved away, Joe sat back, and his eyes narrowed on Alegra. "Are you angry?"

"Should I be?"

He shrugged. It hit her then that she didn't have a clue if he was married or divorced. It appeared he had a child, however. A three-year-old boy. "I could see that you didn't have time for food then," he said.

"You have a short fuse."

"I just don't have time to squeeze substantive questions in between phone calls."

She took a swallow of her gin and tonic before she

leaned toward him and said, "You didn't have to yell 'Whatever' as you disappeared."

He chuckled. "See what I mean? Isn't it the most annoying word in the English dictionary?"

"In the top ten," she admitted as she realized she was starting to relax just a bit. She felt more mellow, and she wasn't sure if it was the drink or his smile.

"How did you know about the parking area near the lighthouse?" he said without any preamble.

"I stumbled on it," she lied, and quickly picked up her menu, opening it to partially block his view of her as she scanned the items. She read them aloud to fill in that space between her and Joe so he wouldn't ask any more questions. When she finished with, "And 'Bloody Jack's Prime Rib,'" she peered over the top of the menu at Joe. "Now, that sounds appetizing, don't you think?"

He was watching her intently. "Seems fitting for this setting."

The waitress showed up with Joe's drink, then took their orders. She couldn't resist the pasta—Mad Patrick's Penne. Joe ordered the prime rib, along with a carafe of red wine.

When the waitress left, Alegra sank back in her seat and looked directly at Joe. "So, let me get this straight. If I take a phone call, you leave, even if you are supposed to be interviewing me for your story, right?"

He seemed to consider that for a moment, then said, "I probably wouldn't, mostly because I'm starving. And I want to do the interview, despite your damn phone."

He could bring that anger up with so little effort! She

lifted her phone. "Look, it's a convenience. It's important in business to stay connected at all times." She lowered it to the table with a sigh. "Forget it. You wouldn't understand."

"Rather condescending of you," he muttered.

"I didn't mean—"

He cut her off. "That's okay. Believe it or not, there was a time when you'd have thought I'd had a cell phone surgically implanted in my hand."

"New York can do that to a person," she murmured.

She didn't miss a certain tightness that crept into his expression. "That was another life," he said.

"But it was yours."

"So is this. This is where I grew up. I left after high school graduation and went out to conquer the world." He paused when the waitress came back with the carafe and he took his time pouring a goblet for Alegra before topping off his own drink. Joe reached for his goblet. He held it up in a salute. "Here's to our lives now, and here's to this place."

She didn't move to touch her own glass. "Was your life in New York that bad?" she asked, discovering she really wanted to know.

He sat back and pressed one hand to the tabletop with splayed fingers. Then he spoke in a low voice. "This is supposed to be about you, not me. I'm the journalist, the one who's supposed to be asking the questions."

"You don't have your notebook with you, and I don't have my press packet with me, so humor me," she said. "Give me a thumbnail sketch of your past life."

"That's the point, it's my *past* life. It's done."

"And forgotten?"

"Do you forget your past?"

"No one does," she said softly. "Our past makes us what we are today." She quickly amended that statement. "Or it drives us to be what we are today." She took a breath, avoiding thoughts of what had made her what she was. "What made you put that life behind you?"

He smiled wryly. "All right, if you insist, I'll give you that thumbnail sketch. I left here, graduated college in journalism and business, moved to New York and started out as an intern at the newspaper. I graduated to writing obituaries, then moved up to community news, the city buzz, and finally made it to the serious news. No overnight sensation, but eventually, I got to near the top, then *to* the top."

He'd been the editor of one of the largest, most respected newspapers in the country and now he was here, doing a weekly paper that had little to no impact on any world but the island?

Alegra couldn't get her mind around it. "So how could you just walk away? Why would anyone choose this place, this life, over everything you had?"

Alegra lifted her gin and tonic, but it was empty. So she took a swallow of wine. As the warmth spread in her, she waited for Joe to answer. He finally did.

"See, you can't believe it," he said frowning. "But I can't believe that it took me so long to do it."

Their food arrived, but Alegra barely glanced at the steaming plate of pasta with its rich, creamy sauce.

Instead, she told him, "All I know is, I would have *never* walked away from the life I've made for myself and come back to this."

"Well," he replied, "sometimes what we think we want turns out to be everything we don't need."

She shook her head. "That's crazy. What's wrong with success, with working for what you want and getting it?"

"Nothing. Nothing at all, unless…" He took a sip of wine. "Everyone has to decide what's most important to them. It's that simple."

Simple. She'd decided a long time ago to get out of here, and she had. She'd decided to be everything she never could have been here, and she was. Was that simple? She shook her head. "It's your choice, and if you're happy…" She let her words trail off as she picked up her fork.

"AND THIS INTERVIEW is supposed to be about you," Joe said. Truth was, he'd been on the verge of forgetting who was interviewing whom and telling her about Jean and the breakup and the day he knew that he only wanted to be here with Alex. But her "It's your choice, and if you're happy" was so pat and so annoyingly condescending—did she make a habit of being condescending?—that he bit back his story. All he said was, "Damn straight," deciding to put off the interview for a bit until he was in a better mood, then tackled his food.

Alegra methodically ate her pasta, sipping wine and occasionally sighing softly, but she didn't make any effort to make more conversation. When Joe decided enough was enough, he put down his utensils and waited for Alegra to look up from her meal.

He wondered if a woman like her could ever understand how priorities could shift and change? He finally said, "The three-year-old is my son, Alex."

Her fork stopped on the way to her mouth, then lowered to the plate with a slight clatter. "I figured that must have been your son." She pulled the napkin off her lap and dropped it over her almost empty plate. "And your wife…?"

"She's gone."

He knew his blunt choice of words was wrong when color touched her cheeks and she murmured, "Oh, I'm so sorry. No wonder you came back and—"

"Oh, no, she's not dead. She's in Zambia, I think."

Her eyes widened. "Zambia?"

"Last I heard."

"What's she doing there?"

"She's working. She's a photographer. Jean Miles."

"The photographer who does all those wild-animal photos?"

She knew of her? "Yup."

"Well, it is a small world," she murmured.

"How so?" he asked.

"I used her work for an ad campaign about six or seven months ago." She sat forward with her elbows on the table and her fingers laced so she could rest her chin on them. "We were starting an animal-print line, and her photos were terrific, African and lush and so sensual."

He thought she might have colored just a bit at her choice of words. "They were great."

He had visions of how Alegra would use the theme of wild animals in her business. "I bet they were."

"So, you're here and she's there, and…?"

"We're divorced," he said bluntly.

"Oh." She took the time to sit back, lift her wine and take a sip before asking, "And you have custody of your son?"

"Yes. I brought him back here, and we're staying with my mother and father. Their house is just down the beach from the lighthouse. That's why I was on the beach earlier. It's where I grew up, my home. You know, the one place you can go back to no matter what happens in your life."

He watched Alegra lower her eyes, those ridiculously long lashes shading her expression, and he thought she whispered, "Sure." Then she looked up, but not at him. She waved to the waitress, who came over to the table. "The bill?" she asked.

The waitress collected their plates, then hurried off. Joe watched Alegra fiddle with a fork that had been left behind, straightening it, then turning it sideways before she righted it again. He could see her discomfort. Not anger, not embarrassment, but something he'd said had bothered her, had put that expression in her eyes, and now she wanted out of here. "It's my treat," he said for lack of anything else to say that would get her to look at him again.

When she glanced up, her eyes held a tinge of bleakness in the amber hue, then she shook her head and reached for her jacket, from which she produced a slim wallet. "No, I'll take care of it," she said quickly, and as the waitress came to the table, she put out a hand to take the bill.

Joe didn't bother arguing. It didn't matter to him. He said, "Thanks," and let her take out a credit card, give it to the waitress, then sit back and wait for the girl to return. "We only talked about me," he said. "I didn't get anything about you."

She looked at him blankly for a moment, then said, "Oh, maybe later we can talk."

The waitress was back, handing her a pen and the receipt. She signed it quickly, and Joe didn't miss the slight unsteadiness in her hand as she added what he could tell was a more than generous tip. Then the waitress was gone, and Alegra was standing, slipping on her leather jacket and pushing her wallet and phone in the pockets. "Thanks for the company," she said and left.

Joe got to his feet and caught up to her as she exited the front entry of the restaurant. The night was cold, and the mist was haloing the lights of the town. He wasn't sure she knew he was there as he came up to her side on the fake gangplank, but when he spoke to her, she didn't seem surprised. "Going back to the Snug Harbor?" he asked.

She stopped, not looking at him, but glancing right and left up the street. "What do they do if it rains on the festival?" she asked without answering his question.

"It's not *if,*" he said, watching her as she looked up

at the blackness of the sky. "It's *when*. And they have tons of canopies and awnings and tents to protect everything." He motioned down the street on the far side where he could make out a sea of those very things for protection by the park. "Rain is part of life here."

She shrugged, her arms hugging herself tightly, but she didn't make a move to go any farther. "How do you live with it?" she asked in a low voice.

He did his own version of answering a question with a question. "Is something wrong? Did I say something that upset you?"

"You? No, it's not you. I've…" She bit her bottom lip, then exhaled a sigh that misted in the cold air. She never looked at him. "I've got work to do."

She would have left, but he touched her on the upper arm. He felt her stiffen, then stand absolutely still in front of him. "No vacation at all while you're here?"

As if to answer his question, there was a muffled ring. Her cell phone again. She pulled it out, looked down at the glowing readout on the front, then hit the ignore button before she spoke to him again. "This isn't a vacation."

A direct answer, yet he thought he caught a certain sadness in it. He had the most overwhelming urge to take the phone and toss it away, then pull the woman to him. But he just said, "Too bad," and meant it.

Chapter Six

When Alegra turned from Joe and started up the street toward the bed-and-breakfast, his words rang in her mind. *You know, the one place you can go back to no matter what happens in your life?*

She walked more quickly through the mist that was changing to a light rain. She would have run if Joe hadn't been somewhere behind her, watching her. Then she sensed movement by her. Joe, falling in step with her. He was quiet as they neared the park entry, obviously with no idea that what he'd said was like a blow to her midsection. *You know, the one place you can go back to no matter what happens in your life?* No, she didn't know. She had never known. She never would.

She barely controlled a trembling that she felt deep inside her, and she hoped Joe would just go away when she got to the bed-and-breakfast. Then she'd be alone.

At last the old Victorian was there. She turned into the driveway and headed for her cottage, and when she reached it and stopped, Joe caught her gently by her upper arm, turned her toward him. She didn't try to break away, but just waited.

He studied her for a long, agonizing moment, then moved closer, dipping his head and she felt instant horror at the idea he was about to kiss her.

But there was no kiss. His lips weren't on hers, but by her ear, and he whispered softly, "Sleep well, and turn off your damn phone."

Then he moved back, withdrawing his touch, and she stared at him, not at all sure why she felt oddly let down. He cocked his head to one side, said, "Call me when you're free to talk," and headed off into the misty night.

She went into her cottage, stripped off her damp clothes and turned on the shower. As soon as the water heated up, she stepped under the warmth.

His words came back to her. *You know, the one place you can go back to no matter what happens in your life?* In that moment, she thought she could hate Joe Lawrence. He *had* that one place. She never had. She slapped the tiled wall with the flat of her hand and wept.

ALEGRA AWOKE the next morning to the sound of a marching band playing "The Star Spangled Banner." She pushed herself to a sitting position. Despite the fact the noise literally made the air around her vibrate, the band wasn't in her bedroom. The sound came over loudspeakers, probably from the nearby park.

She glanced at the clock and groaned. After a night of self-pity, she hadn't fallen asleep until the wee hours. She reached for a terry robe to put on over the faded

T-shirt she slept in. An incongruous choice of nightwear for a woman who designed fabulous lingerie, Alegra recognized, but comfortable all the same.

She crossed to open the door and look outside. It wasn't raining, but the ever present mist was in place. Through the mist came the music, along with people cheering and clapping. She closed the door. "Opening ceremonies," she muttered.

As she splashed her face with cool water, she could hear a brassy rendition of "Whiskey Johnnie." "Debauchery," she said to her reflection in the mirror. She almost smiled at the thought of Joe giving his definition of debauchery.

She quickly dressed in jeans, a heavy cable-knit sweater and her boots. She'd contact Joe later to talk; she'd give him her press packet and a few facts about her business. There wouldn't be any reason to see him again after she gave him her version of success.

Alegra pulled her hair up and away from her face in a ponytail. She had work to do, contacts to make, a phone call or two she should put through, but she found that the idea of doing any of it was about as appealing as the world outside that seemed to be comprised of one huge brass band. She looked around the living area, then decided to climb in the car and drive away from the cacophony for a while. She reached for her keys and wallet, and as she turned to retrieve her cell phone from a table by the door, she stopped.

She hadn't noticed it before, but Sean Payne's painting, delivered the previous afternoon and put inside, was propped against the wall by the table. The top of the lighthouse was visible above the brown-paper wrapping. She hunkered down in front of it, still in awe of how Sean had captured the feeling of the location with a minimum of brush strokes.

She reached out and pulled the paper back to expose more of the canvas. When Joe had found her yesterday at the lighthouse, her plan for her stay on Shelter Island had been to see her family's old house, take care of the sale, then donate a very large sum at the festival ball into a general fund for restoration of the town and island. She hadn't really cared what, precisely, the money was used for, just that people knew who'd given it.

Now that plan had changed. She was going to earmark her donation for the restoration of the old lighthouse. And then she'd make sure that the fund for upkeep wouldn't go dry. The lighthouse beacon would be reactivated and stay that way. No one else would have to imagine the light the way she had when she was a kid. As apparently the tortured artist Sean had become had imagined it.

She grabbed a jacket, not the leather one, but a navy rain-proof, hooded windbreaker. When she stepped outside, the sounds of the celebration rushed at her on the cold, wet air.

Minutes later she was in her car and on the road heading north, impeded by the crush of vehicles heading to the festival. The mist turned to rain and she turned on her windshield wipers. She passed the newspaper office, saw a sign on the door, Gone To Celebrate, and kept going, mindful of pedestrians, many of whom treated the festival like Mardi Gras, swarming all over the streets, not bothering to check for cars. Some were dressed in pirate costumes, and the need for umbrellas didn't seem to dampen their spirits in the least.

She finally made it out of town, putting the colorful sights and sounds behind her, and took the same road she'd taken to the lighthouse the day before. As she passed some scattered houses, she wondered offhandedly if any of them were Joe's parents'. She'd never really known where the Lawrences lived when she'd lived here. She'd never cared.

She passed the turnoff for the clearing where she'd parked to visit the lighthouse. Staying on the same road, she literally circled the island until she was on the far western side, approaching Bent River, the only other town on the island, which she'd seldom visited as a child. It still consisted of only three or four houses, a few peach orchards, a gas station, a small restaurant and a general store, none of the expansion that Shelter Bay had enjoyed.

When at last she reached the ferry landing, she slowed, swung a U-turn and went back the way she'd come. As she drove, she put in a call to Roz to tell her to contact the committee who arranged her original donation and change the conditions of usage for the money. When she hung up, she spotted the restaurant in Bent River and went in for lunch. After lingering over coffee and dessert, she finally left and kept driving. She looked ahead and caught a glimpse of the top of the lighthouse over the massive trees.

This time she pulled into the clearing on the bluffs and stayed in the car with the engine running and heater blowing warm air. There was no place to go on the island. No place to just forget and relax. No place to wander. Every place was her past, butting up against her with agonizing consistency. Cocooned in the car, she knew she didn't want to go back to the town and the festival. She no longer wanted to drive around, either, going in circles and getting nowhere. And finding Joe would be hopeless. He could be anywhere, and probably with his son.

Finally, she turned off the car and got out, taking her keys and phone. She went down to the beach, then walked slowly toward the water's edge.

The mainland was almost lost in the grayness and rain. A distant place. A place she thought of as the promised land, when, as a child, she'd sat here looking out across the water, pretending the beam from the lighthouse could show it to her. It seemed fitting now to donate her money to get the light actually lit.

"Hey, there!" Startled, she turned to see Joe approaching and a little boy playing on the sand behind him. Her heart raced for a moment. "I called this time," he said as he came closer. "Didn't want you to think I was sneaking up on you."

He had on a yellow slicker, but the hood was pushed back and his hair gleamed with droplets of rain. "Are you following me?" she asked, forcing a smile

JOE FLINCHED slightly at her question. All he knew for sure was that he was glad she was here, and he liked looking at her.

He offered her a wry smile in return. "I thought maybe *you* were following *me,* and tried to throw me off by getting here first and waiting for me to show up."

"That makes no sense," she murmured.

"I know," he admitted. "I was going for a joke, but it didn't make it, did it?"

Her smile looked even more forced. "No, it didn't."

"Too bad," he said, suddenly not at all sure he could ever make her really smile, and jealous of the man who could. "So, what are you doing here again?" he asked.

"It's too crazy in town. I was going to get in touch with you and see if you had time for that interview, but the office was closed, so I went for a drive. But driving around here just brings you back where you started."

He chuckled. "Yeah, you can only go so far before you start repeating yourself."

"Got it! I got it!"

His son was rushing along the beach toward them, his rubber boots slapping on the hard sand and his yellow slicker flapping around him. His pale blond hair ruffled in the breeze and his face was flushed with excitement.

"See, I winned." Alex held a wiggling crab in his hand. "I got it."

The excitement in the three-year-old suddenly turned to something akin to shyness. He stopped three feet or so from them, fell silent and stared at Alegra. The crab was twisting to get free.

Joe knew that parents always thought their kids were perfect, but Alex, sweet-natured and bright, with deep blue eyes set in a face that was almost angelic, was truly perfect, everything a parent would ever want in a child. Joe was deeply in love with him.

He could never understand how Jean had been able to just walk away, with only a few phone calls here and there, and just a single visit a year ago. And the longer it went with Jean not demanding anything more, the more easily Joe breathed.

Now Alex was here with him, on a beach, with Alegra, and showing her his prize crab. "I winned," he said again in a small voice.

"What did you win?" Alegra asked, keeping a wary eye on the wild crustacean.

Alex grinned. "I winned a nickel." He looked at Joe. "Right, Daddy?"

"Right."

"He's a great crab!" Alex said, his excitement returning, and without warning, he lunged toward Alegra with the infuriated crab in tow. Alegra stumbled backward in her attempt to evade contact with the crustacean and fell to the sand on her backside. Alex was so startled he let go of the crab—and it landed right in the middle of Alegra's chest.

Both Alex and Alegra screamed, but for totally different reasons. Alex was alarmed, but Alegra was horrified. She swiped frantically at the crab without success. So Joe took over, crouching above Alegra, and plucking the hapless crab from her chest and returning it to Alex. Alegra scooted backward, her face flushed and her eyes never leaving the flailing crab in his son's hand.

"Take it away," she said in a breathless voice. "Just get it out of here."

"It's okay," Joe said as he got to his feet, then helped Alegra to hers. "It's under control."

She glared at him, then brushed at her pants as she muttered, "I hate those things."

"They're delicious," Joe said.

She gave him another glare. "Steamed I can take. Mean and nasty and alive, I can't." She flashed a look at Alex, who seemed oblivious to her discomfort, and her voice was less harsh when she spoke to him. "Please, get that thing out of here."

"Okay, okay," Joe said, resigned, and turned to take the crab from Alex. Then he crossed to a grouping of rocks, released the crustacean and watched it scurry into the protection of the nearest crevice. He walked back to Alegra, who was brushing at her bottom now.

"What a mess," she complained.

"I think the poor crab got the worst of it."

"How do you figure that?" she asked. "Because your son threw it at me?"

"Alex was just offering you a closer look."

"I never asked for one," she said, obviously still upset.

Joe decided it was time for a proper introduction. "Alex," he said, touching his son on the shoulder, "this is Ms. Reynolds." He shifted his gaze to Alegra. "This is my son, Alex, the great crab hunter."

Alegra looked at his little boy, but maintained her distance. "Nice to meet you, Alex."

"I'm sorry," Alex said without prompting. Joe felt a rush of pride.

"No problem," Alegra said without much conviction in her voice.

"He got scared," the boy said.

"He wasn't the only one," she responded wryly.

"Well, he's gone now, Alegra," Joe said, "unless you want me to go after him and get him for your dinner?"

She shook her head and sighed. "And all I wanted was some peace and quiet."

Joe heard this as a rebuke, as if he and Alex had broken that peace and quiet for her, which, he admitted, they probably had. He touched Alex on the shoulder again. "Let's get going so the lady can have her peace and quiet."

"Oh, no, I didn't mean that," she said quickly. "I just meant that the craziness in town is just too much…and then the crab…"

"Alex, go and look for another crab, but stay in sight, and no going in the water." As the boy darted away, Joe called after him, "And no climbing!"

Joe turned to Alegra. "Tomorrow things should be calmer. A wine tasting in the afternoon helps things mellow out." He couldn't resist adding, "You know, general debauchery."

She gave the faintest suggestion of a genuine smile, and his groin tightened. Damn it, he should have left with Alex. Despite his desire to see her really smile, he knew that he probably shouldn't be anywhere nearby when it happened.

"There's one thing I just don't get about you," he said. "You're here, at the busiest, noisiest time of the year, but you don't want any part of it."

She nibbled on her bottom lip, then shrugged. "So, I'm not into debauchery."

Another answer that didn't tell him anything. "What *are* you into, Alegra Reynolds?"

"Well, not crabs, that's for sure." She turned and looked over at Alex, who was tugging on a tangled mess of seaweed. "You said his mother's in Africa?"

She'd deflected another question and Joe sighed inwardly. "Yeah, Zambia," he said bitterly, "probably taking pictures of baby elephants or giraffes, but I don't think she has more than two or three pictures of Alex." Why in hell had he told her *that?* "But it's her choice."

Joe didn't miss the way she rotated her head as if freeing up tension in her neck muscles. "Just because she gave birth to him, doesn't make her a mother," she said.

That simplicity stunned him. The truth was there, laid bare between them. Jean had given birth to Alex, but had never been a mother to him. "Some people should never have children," he said for lack of any other point of wisdom.

"Too bad you never know who should or shouldn't until it's too late," she said softly. Was that a tinge of pain he saw in her eyes? "And the child doesn't have any say in it or any choices."

He knew she couldn't possibly know Jean's short-comings, beyond what he'd told her, and he sensed her words weren't even about his ex-wife. "Exactly," he replied, "and Jean's choice was work."

"You make work sound like a four-letter word," Alegra murmured.

He laughed. "Lady, work *is* a four-letter word. Literally."

There was nothing for a moment, then in a sudden burst, he got his wish. Her smile came out full force. It dimpled her cheeks, flushed her skin and made her eyes shine. He could barely breathe as he watched her.

"Touché," she said, the words mingling with her own laughter.

He pushed his hands into his pockets, and although he turned his gaze to his son, who was digging furiously into the wet sand at the water's edge, all he really saw was that smile. And his brain was racing through other four-letter words. Need. Want. Lust. He stopped it there and moved away, jogging toward Alex as he tried to think of a four-letter word for crazy.

He couldn't think of one.

Chapter Seven

Alegra felt as if she'd stepped into a parallel universe that was tipping in the oddest direction. She was talking about mothers with Joe and had stopped him leaving, so she was now on the beach with him and a three-year-old boy whose jewel-like blue eyes matched his father's perfectly. She watched Joe crouch by Alex and put his arm around the child.

She'd never thought about kids, never chose to be around them. Yet here she was feeling an ache in her middle for a little boy whose mother didn't want him. A child who was digging in the sand as if his life depended on it while his father held on to him.

She could have just left. But instead, she moved closer to the two of them. She saw that Alex had captured another crab, a smaller one, but one just as angry at being trapped as the other crab had been. The child's tiny hand had a firm grip on the shell, and the pincers flashed in the air in erratic swipes.

"Whoa," Joe said, taking the crab from Alex and

staring down at it. "This one's nice, really nice." He glanced at Alegra, then held the crab up for her to see, but didn't push it toward her at all. "What do you think?"

"Impressive," she said, not going any closer.

Alex clapped with glee. "I winned, I winned again!"

"You sure did." Joe put the crab down and for one horrible moment she was sure the critter was going to make a beeline for her. But then it scurried back between Joe's boots and into the water and was gone.

"Smart crab," she murmured and didn't miss the flash of a smile as Joe stood by her.

"He'll be dinner for someone sooner or later," he said.

"You know," she said, "I'm rethinking. Maybe I'll stop eating seafood altogether."

Joe's chuckle sent a tiny frisson of pleasure through her. "If you see a bull with horns," he said, "are you swearing off beef?"

She smiled. "I'll just avoid bulls."

Alex tugged on his father's slicker. "More, Daddy, please?"

"Sure, one more, but let's go farther down the beach. The crabs here need a break from terrorism for a while."

"Okay," the boy said, then took off.

Joe motioned in the direction Alex had gone. "Coming?"

Of course not, she should have said, but just nodded and fell in step beside him.

She heard him take a breath before saying, "So, let's get started on the piece for the paper."

"You don't have a notebook, and I don't have my press release with me again," she said.

"I've got an excellent memory, so no notebook needed, and I don't want to see your press release. This is a 'human interest' story, so it's about the human part, not the smoke and mirrors."

Smoke and mirrors? "It's just the facts, not fiction," she said, staring straight ahead of them.

"Okay, I'll check it out later. For now, let's start at the beginning. Where did you grow up?"

"My childhood isn't important," she said, at the same time seeing this man's son thrilled to be on the beach with his dad hunting for crabs. His childhood would be important when he grew up. He'd remember it with a smile. She clenched her hands into fists in her pockets.

"What's the old saying that our past makes our present possible?"

"Very philosophical," she murmured. Her past had made her what she was, but it was *despite* her past, not because of it.

"That's as deep as I get," he said. "So let's keep it basic. Where did it all start?"

She squinted into the distance. She could absolutely tell him where the part of her past she *valued* had started—the moment she got to her grandmother's house. "South of San Francisco." It had been a tiny house in a low-income area, but it had been a true sanctuary for her when she'd arrived right after high school graduation. "I was there until I graduated from college."

"How about your parents?" he asked.

"My father…he did odd jobs, this and that." Between his drinking binges. "What about yours?" she asked, hoping to move on and get away from family questions before he got to her mother.

It seemed to work. "Dad worked in Seattle for years as an aircraft developer," Joe said. "Mom was just here, you know, home when you left, home when you got home. Back then it didn't seem that important, but now, I know it was everything."

She couldn't control a violent shudder. Having a mother like Joe had would have been like a fairy tale to her back then. "It's so damn cold," she muttered, tucking her chin into her jacket collar.

They strolled nearer Alex, determinedly stacking debris and loose rocks into a pyramid of sorts by the cliff, the crabs forgotten. Joe stopped by a large rock and leaned against it, the breeze lifting his hair.

She'd never been one to look at a man and have any thoughts of what-ifs. But she did now. What if Joe and she had met someplace else? What if he wasn't tied to this place, and what if she didn't hate this place? What if they were on neutral ground, equals in what they wanted, just two people getting to know each other?

She felt her stomach tighten sickeningly as reality intruded. There was just this. Here and now. And that wouldn't change. She looked away from the man and out to the water again, walking slowly to the spot where waves lapped the sand. "How long do you think the festivities will go on in town?" she asked.

"For days," Joe said. His voice, right behind her,

startled her, and she turned suddenly, nearly falling, but he had her by her upper arm. His hand slid slowly up to her shoulder, then rested there. "I should've whistled to let you know I was behind you."

She stared at him. He was so damn sexy. Those blue eyes, the slight curl of his longish dark hair, that muscular physique. Her reaction was disturbing, and she faked a shiver to break the contact. "It's just me. This place makes me…" She closed her eyes for a moment. "I don't know. Jumpy, I guess." She knew it wasn't entirely the place that put her nerves on edge.

"Odd. Most people say it's peaceful. That they like the calm and tranquility here." His eyes narrowed. "But then again, they usually come here to relax."

She walked over to the little boy and hunkered down beside the pile of things he'd made. She tried to blot out his father, so near to her. "I bet I know what this is."

"What?" Alex asked, his blue eyes on her.

She touched some seaweed that he'd laid over rocks and pieces of wood. "It's a trap. You build it, and when the tide comes in and the water flows behind it, it wears away the sand and leaves a hole." She smoothed the seaweed back into place. "And if you're lucky, the hole gets really deep. When you come back later on, there'll be things in the hole, not aware they're in a trap…like crabs."

He clapped his hands. "Yeah!" he said. "Crabs!"

"So I'm right?" The boy's wide smile touched something deep inside her.

"Yes!"

She stood as Alex happily grabbed more seaweed and

rocks to put in place. From behind her, Joe asked, "How did you know that? About the dam and the hole?"

Because that was how she'd played as a child all alone. She remembered coming back to the same spot on the beach over and over again, seeing the hole get bigger and bigger, thinking if she did it enough, maybe the hole would open up and she'd fall through it to another world like Alice in Wonderland. "I did it sometimes as a kid," she said. "One time four crabs were in my hole, and I made the mistake of trying to carry them all at once." She'd thought if she took them home for her dad that he'd be happy and they could cook them and be a normal family for a little while. She'd been wrong. "They all bit me," she said with a grimace.

"Didn't anyone ever tell you to only carry them one at a time?"

"No." She squinted at the sky. "It's going to rain again."

"Seems so," he said, then spoke to his son. "We need to go back, Alex."

The boy acted as if he hadn't heard. He kept pushing stones into the pile, making it wider and higher.

"Alex?"

"Gotta finish," he said breathlessly as he dumped more rocks on the pile.

To her surprise, Joe didn't simply pick up his son and cart him away. Instead, he squatted down, reached for some stones, and helped make the dam wider and higher. Finally, he stood up and swiped his hands back and forth. "Okay, now we have to go. If you make it any bigger, the water can't get around it, and there won't be a hole at all and the dam will wash away. There won't be any crabs."

Magic words, she thought as the boy stood quickly and mimicked his father's hand-cleaning action. "Okay," he said, grinning. Then he shot off, running down the beach, weaving toward the water, then back toward the cliffs again and again.

Joe started after his son and she walked along beside. "You've got good instincts with kids," she said.

"No, it's not instincts," he replied. "It's learned. At first, I couldn't even hold him. He scared me to death, all seven pounds of him."

"What were you scared of?"

She slanted him a glance and saw he was watching Alex ahead of them. "I used the excuse that he was too tiny and I'd break him." He paused. "But then I figured it out. I just didn't want him."

That stopped her in her tracks. He stopped, too, and turned to her. "You didn't want him?" The admission didn't fit the man she knew.

"No, I didn't." Joe was dead serious. "He was an accident. My wife and I were about to separate and she got pregnant, so we agreed to stay together until she had the baby, then see what we would do."

She almost gasped. Her parents had married because her mother had been pregnant. She'd been told that often enough, that she'd never been wanted, and she was sure everyone on the island knew. It made her physically ache to think that the boy with the face of a cherub hadn't been wanted, either.

Alex laughed right then as he chased a piece of paper fluttering across the sand. "How could you not want him?" she asked.

Joe released a breath on a low hiss. "Yeah, how could I not? He was perfect. A beautiful baby. My son. I should have loved him on sight. I didn't."

"Do you love him now?"

"Oh, yes. I can't even begin to tell you how much. But that didn't happen until he was probably six months old, and one day, just like that, when my wife told me that she was leaving, I knew I didn't want *him* to leave. I wanted him with me. She didn't seem to care, but I wanted him to be happy and safe and loved."

His words produced a profound sense of despair in her. To be loved like that. She'd never known it and doubted she ever would. She tried to push away thoughts of her own mother leaving. She'd been six, and she'd known all about it. Alex had been too young to have a memory in his mind of her walking out. "He's so lucky to have you," she said simply.

Emotion roughened Joe's voice when he spoke again. "My mother always said that everybody deserves to have one person in this life who smiles when they enter a room. Alex deserves much more than that."

One person who smiled when you walked in the room? One person who wasn't on your payroll or had their own agenda? Just one person. She didn't have anyone.

JOE KNEW THAT, once again, he'd said something that bothered her. He'd talked about personal things when he was supposed to be extracting information from her. She stopped at the tide line, her arms hugged around herself and the growing breeze playing with her hair. He thought she was staring into the distance, but when he moved closer he saw that her eyes were shut and her bottom lip caught by even white teeth.

"Cold?" he asked. When she nodded, he finished with, "Being from San Francisco, you should be accustomed to damp cold."

She didn't respond for a moment, then her eyes opened and she ran a hand over her face. "It's not like it is here." She turned around and walked past him. "I need to get back."

He called after her, "Would you have dinner with me again? I mean tonight. I know about another place that won't be full." He motioned with a hand vaguely down the beach. "Mainlanders don't know about it."

She seemed to consider his offer. He hoped she'd agree. Maybe he'd get more information for his newspaper article. "Is the food good?" she asked, taking a step toward him. He had hope.

"Nothing really fancy, but good."

"We won't have to wait in line?"

"Absolutely not."

She glanced down at her clothes. "Do I need to change?"

"No," he said, thinking she'd look good in those jeans

and jacket anywhere. She'd probably look good in a paper bag—or out of it. The thought made him smile.

She eyed him with her head tilted slightly. "What's so funny?"

There was no way he'd tell her. "I'm just happy, that's all."

"Okay, okay," she said doubtfully. "I'll get my car and meet you. Just give me directions."

She probably thought he needed time to take Alex home first. "You don't have to," he said. "It's not far. Right up there, a terrific view of the sound, and some really good wine to boot."

"Now, you're intriguing me," she said. He wished that was true on every level.

"Great," he said. "Let's go."

They caught up with Alex, who darted ahead again. The two of them walked side by side, not stopping till they reached a set of narrow stairs farther down the beach. Joe motioned to them for Alegra. "Up there," he said. Joe stood back with Alex to let Alegra go up first. When he and his son reached the top step, Alegra stood in the high grass of the bluff looking at his house.

The bungalow looked welcoming, Joe thought. Light spilled out the lower windows onto the wraparound porch, and smoke curled out of the stone chimney into the evening air. Alex was already at the porch steps, scrambling up them, when the door flew open and he disappeared inside.

Joe touched Alegra on the arm. "Come on," he said.

They stepped up onto the porch. He opened the door

and motioned her inside. Following her, he heard his mother greet Alex. "Hello, there, big boy!" Her voice came through the air at the same time Alex giggled. "And hello to you, too," his mother said. Joe moved closer and saw his mom speaking to Alegra, who had stopped in front of him in the doorway between the kitchen and the mud room.

"Hello," Alegra said.

"Don't tell me you found Alex and—"

Then she spotted Joe over Alegra's shoulder. "There you are," she said, and Joe was struck by how tiny his mother was, especially holding Alex on one hip. Barely five feet tall, maybe a hundred pounds, she had a delicate look. But that was deceptive. She was as strong as any woman he'd ever known.

"Mom, this is Alegra Reynolds. We met by the old lighthouse."

Alex squirmed to get down, and his grandmother put him on the floor. As the little boy ran from the kitchen into the living area, Joe started to say something about Alegra, to explain who she was, but that was taken out of his hands.

"Well," his mom said, smiling, "Joey's brought home a lot of strays in his time, but bringing home Alegra Reynolds has gotta be at the top of the list." She moved closer and stuck out her hand. "Alegra's Closet? Are you *that* Alegra? I heard you were in town at the Snug Harbor."

"I wasn't aware my presence would create any stir," Alegra said.

"Oh, my, yes. This is a treat. I love your bath-oil line,

and those lace teddies—so gorgeous, especially the ones in taupe with the ribbon straps."

Joe couldn't believe his ears. His mother? The woman who wore jeans and shirts? Whose nightgowns were full-length flannel affairs? He cleared his throat and touched the small of Alegra's back, urging her into the kitchen. "Mother, you never cease to amaze me."

"I might be a grandma, but that doesn't mean I'm over the hill. At least, your father doesn't think so."

No, he would not go down that road, even if his mother *was* still a pretty woman and his dad a remarkably fit sixty-six-year-old. "Okay, okay," he said with a laugh. "I believe you."

"So, Joey met you on the beach?" she asked Alegra. "Let me have your jacket."

While his mother hung it on one of the pegs by the door, Alegra said, "I wanted to see the lighthouse." As Joe took off his slicker and boots, her amber eyes turned to him. "This is it, isn't it?"

He nodded. He'd thought she might not come with him if she'd known the eating place was his home. "The food's great," he said, uneasily waiting for her response.

He needn't have worried. A small smile curved her lips. "And no lineup as you promised," she said.

He didn't let himself release a huge sigh of relief.

Alex blasted back into the room just then, making a beeline for Alegra. Before he could stop him, the boy had his arms around her legs, looking up at her. "Come see Mr. Melon, please?"

She hunkered down to his level. "Mr. Melon?"

"Uh-huh," Alex said. He grabbed her hand and started tugging her.

She looked up at Joe. "Mr. Melon?"

"It's his cat," he said.

She gave Joe a long look, then said, "No lineup, just a cat," and then she smiled. A wide, blinding, genuine smile.

When she left the kitchen with his son, he heard her voice trailing back through the open door. "Oh, nice to meet you, Mr. Melon."

He was startled when his mom slapped him on the arm. "Joe, what's the story? Alegra of Alegra's Closet, coming home with you?" She was grinning. "What's been going on that I don't know about? And I need details, all the details."

He glanced at the doorway, then back at his mother. "I'm doing an interview, a human-interest piece about her stay on the island, what brought her here."

"Is she here alone?"

"Yes."

"Married?"

"No."

"Divorced?"

"I don't think so." He held up his hand. "Tell you what, Mother, you can do the interview and I'll just take notes."

Christina laughed and shook her head. "Well, son, if you're around her and only want to take notes, I need to have a long talk with you."

The sound of Alegra's laughter filtered in from the

other room. He knew at that moment that he had never really wanted an interview with Alegra. That wasn't even on the list of what he wanted with her.

Chapter Eight

Alegra was still in the parallel universe she'd fallen into on the beach. But now she, Alegra Reynolds, was sitting at a huge dining table with the three-year-old, who was eating spaghetti one strand at a time and getting more sauce on his face and hands than in his mouth. The child's father was across the table from her, smiling at her when their eyes met, and the man's parents were friendlier than any people she'd ever met in her life.

On top of all of that, the bucolic scene was actually taking place on Shelter Island!

It was as if she was being given a glimpse of the life she'd longed for but never had. The family dinner, nobody drunk, the doting grandparents with the child, their son across the table, and her sitting in the middle of it all just soaking it in. She lifted her glass to sip some wine when she realized Joe's father was speaking to her. Joe Senior was the image of his son, just thirty years older. The blue eyes were still direct and filled with questions.

"So what do you think of our island?" he was asking.

She put down her glass and evaded any direct response. "The island is really a different way of life, isn't it?"

"It sure is," Joe Senior said, obviously taking her statement as a compliment. "Joey learned the hard way that the world out there isn't a nice place."

"Dad—" Joe smiled indulgently at his father "—I'm sure Alegra doesn't want to hear all about your views on the big bad world."

"Okay, okay, but let's drink a toast." He raised his wineglass. "To the invaders here for the festival. May they not come back for another year." He flashed a grin at Alegra. "Present company excluded."

Alegra managed a smile, even though she heard the man's voice from the past asking if she was okay, right when he'd been protecting her from Sean.

"Hear, hear," his wife said, lifting her glass.

"I really should apologize for just landing on you like this. Joe said he knew a place that had great food." She looked at the man opposite her. "That was the truth, but he failed to say it wasn't a restaurant."

Christina smiled at Alegra. "We're happy to have you here. Though I guess it's not what you're used to, is it?"

"No, but it's delightful," Alegra replied. And the ambience was warm and homey and made her feel almost desperately lonely at the thought of leaving.

Alex dropped his spoon on the floor. When Joe bent to get it, the little boy grabbed at his daddy with spaghetti-sauce-stained hands, leaving a smear of sauce down the back of his father's shirt and into his hair.

Alegra found herself holding her breath, waiting for the anger, especially when Joe jerked up so quickly.

But she had no more reason to brace herself for what Joe would do with the boy than she'd had on the beach earlier. For Joe, after touching his head, actually chuckled at the sauce clinging to his fingers. "What a waste of perfectly good marinara sauce," he said, then stood. "Excuse me while I go and repair the damage." He grinned at Alegra, making her heart lurch. "Just let me warn you to stay clear of him. He's fast and he's no respecter of persons." With that, Joe left the room.

His mother was on her feet, too, going around to Alex and reaching for a napkin to wipe his little hands. "We need to make sure our hands are clean before we use them for anything," she said firmly, but Alegra didn't miss the twitch of her lips. Christina swiped at his face before dropping the napkin on the table. "Now, that's better," she said.

She handed Alex a piece of garlic bread and sank back in her chair. As Alegra watched the little boy chew, she wondered how some children could be so loved, and some never knew what it was like.

"You sound so sad," Christina said to Alegra.

"Excuse me?" Alegra laid down her napkin.

"You sighed, and it sounded as if…" Christina smiled softly. "You must be tired."

Alegra grabbed the excuse. "Yes, I am very tired," she said and got to her feet. "Thank you for everything. It's been lovely." She glanced from the man to the woman. "You've been very kind to a stranger."

"You're not a stranger, not anymore," Joe Senior said. He stood. "And now that we've met, you're welcome here any time at all." He stopped, studied her, then with a slight shake of his head, he said, "If you want to get away from that world out there, remember, we're here."

The warmth and kindness only made it harder for her to breathe, and she moved quickly, going toward the door to get her jacket off the hook. She turned back to say, "Please tell Joe—"

"Tell me what?" Joe asked as he strode into the room, all cleaned up.

"Alegra's tired, and she's leaving," his mother said.

Joe crossed to her and reached around her to get his jacket. "I'll walk you back to your car," he said without giving her a chance to object. "You be good for Mamaw," he said to Alex, then nodded to his dad and mother. "I'll be back in a while."

"Don't rush," his dad called after him.

"You don't have to walk me back," she said when they were outside in the foggy chill air.

Joe shrugged. "Of course I do. First of all, you might get lost, and secondly, I need a favor."

She pulled her jacket tightly around herself. "You're going to get that interview sometime or another so—?"

"It's not that. I need a ride into town."

She followed him off the porch. "Sure, of course, but won't you be stuck there without your truck?"

"My truck's at the office. When I left earlier, my truck was blocked by other cars, so I hitched a ride back." She fell into step with him. "I figure the crowds will be thinning out now, and the cars will be mostly gone."

He preceded her down the steps to the beach below.

At the bottom, they walked in silence along the beach, back the way they'd come. The fog thickened around them, and Alegra could hear the low, mournful sound of foghorns far off in the distance. She felt as if she and Joe were the only two people in the world. For a crazy moment, it was an appealing illusion, then she pushed it aside. She didn't live in illusions. She didn't need them or want them.

"Your father has a poor opinion of the outside world, doesn't he?" she said to Joe.

"He's always had." Joe's voice was low and rough in the night. "When I first went to New York, he had a bet with a friend of his that I'd be back in six months." He chuckled. "He lost the bet."

"But you came back."

"Yes, eventually, and I'm happy I did."

She hunched her shoulders. Of course he was happy here. He had a family that loved him. A little boy. Friends.

"How about you?" he asked. "Happy?"

She'd never made happiness a criterion for anything in her life. She was taken aback to realize that being happy was almost a foreign concept to her. "Things are good," she said evasively, tension starting in her neck again.

The rest of the trip back to the stairs that led up to the clearing where she'd left her car was made in silence. As they stepped into the clearing and headed toward her car, she saw white writing all over the

The Harlequin Reader Service® — Here's how it works:

Get FREE BOOKS and FREE GIFTS when you play the...

LAS VEGAS GAME

7

Just scratch off the gold box with a coin. Then check below to see the gifts you get!

YES! I have scratched off the gold box. Please send me my **2 FREE BOOKS** and **2 FREE GIFTS** for which I qualify. I understand that I am under no obligation to purchase any books as explained on the back of this card.

354 HDL EL32   154 HDL ELUF

FIRST NAME	LAST NAME

ADDRESS

APT.#	CITY

STATE/PROV.	ZIP/POSTAL CODE

(H-AR-05/07)

7	7	7	Worth TWO FREE BOOKS plus TWO BONUS Mystery Gifts!
🍒	🍒	🍒	Worth TWO FREE BOOKS!
🔔	🔔	☘	TRY AGAIN!

www.eHarlequin.com

Offer limited to one per household and not valid to current Harlequin American Romance® subscribers. All orders subject to approval.

▼ DETACH AND MAIL CARD TODAY! ▼

© 2001 HARLEQUIN ENTERPRISES LTD. ® and ™ are trademarks owned and used by the trademark owner and/or its licensee.

tinted windows. Moving closer, she read aloud the words that started on the driver's side window, went back, around the rear of the car and all the way up the windshield.

"Old Bartholomew was here! Beware, matey, beware!"

She heard Joe chuckling as he followed her, then he touched the writing in the last "beware." It smeared. "At least it's done in soap, so with some rain, you'll be bubbling right along."

She climbed in the driver's side, and as Joe settled in the passenger seat, she started the engine. She pushed the button on the windshield wipers and cleaner squirted out. The next instant the wipers slapped from side to side, and she found herself laughing at the results. Bubbles were everywhere. Laughter rose in her, and held more than a bit of hysteria in it.

The laughter rolled out of her until it was coming out in gulps that sounded precariously close to sobs. She felt Joe's hand on her shoulder, and his voice was low in the dim interior. "Hey, it wasn't that funny."

It wasn't, and she knew that the soap writing and bubbles didn't account for her feelings. She just felt so lost, so totally lost. She didn't know how to be happy, and she felt a loss for something that had never been. Her laughter changed to tears.

With a low, "Hey, it's okay," Joe gathered her to him across the console. She buried her face in the rough denim of his jacket and was certain she felt his heart beating against her forehead. He didn't speak, just gently rubbed her back as he rested his chin on the top of her head. He held her, anchoring her, giving her a connection that was so foreign to her and so wonderful, that her sobs only deepened.

JOE HAD NO IDEA what had just happened, but the woman in his arms sounded heartbroken. She held on to him and pressed her face hard into his chest. He hadn't seen this coming. She'd looked sad from time to time, but those moments were brief and were gone almost before he knew they had happened.

But this wasn't brief at all. She stayed in his arms, and even though her sobs died, she still trembled against him. He'd never been comfortable with a woman in tears, and this wasn't an exception, but for the first time, he genuinely wanted to know why she cried.

"It's all right," he whispered against her hair. "It's all right."

He felt her take an unsteady breath, then she was moving away. "Oh, God," she breathed, "I'm so…so sorry."

Then she looked up at him in the dim light of the car, and he could see the dampness on her cheeks and her lashes spiked from her tears. "Tell me what's wrong," he said.

She released a breath in a soft rush. "I don't know," she whispered. "I'm just…"

He shifted, cupping her chin and tipping up her head so she had to look at him. "Just talk to me. Tell me what's going on. I'm a good listener."

She hesitated, seemed on the verge of saying something, but then closed her mouth and lowered her gaze. "I don't…I can't."

"Off the record," he said. He brushed at her damp cheek with his thumb and felt her shiver at the contact. Then she was looking up at him again, and her lips parted softly. He felt a staggeringly strong impulse to kiss her, and when he saw her tongue touch her upper lip, he didn't think twice about bringing his mouth to hers.

Heat and saltiness were there, and her hands were on his chest, but she didn't push him away. Slowly, ever so slowly, her arms lifted and circled his neck. As his tongue tasted her, she came closer. With a low moan, she arched toward him, and even though the console between them dug into his hip, he felt her breasts against his chest. Whatever had stirred him moments ago when she'd been crying, whatever it was that he couldn't define, had changed. He understood what stirred in him now. Understood it completely.

He wanted her. The need to touch her was overwhelming. But as his hands found their way under her jacket to splay on her back, she tensed and drew back, and all he could do was to let her go.

Turning from him, she gripped the steering wheel. The deep shadows in the car blurred her expression. His body ached, and he felt a loss that almost choked him. But he kept quiet and watched her run a hand across her lips before she whispered, "Sorry," and reached to start the ignition.

He sat back, hoping his body would realize sooner, rather than later, that nothing else was going to happen.

He pressed his hands to his thighs as she put the car in gear, then backed out onto the road and turned in the direction of town. He looked out the side window, not wanting to see the vulnerable curve of her throat or the way she was nibbling on her lip again.

The fog was thinner now, and it was raining, coming down hard, and the bubbles on the windows were washed off. The car rocked from the force of the wind.

"More rain," he heard Alegra whisper. "More damn rain."

He turned to her then, tried to think of what to say. He settled for, "I meant it. If you want to talk, I'll listen."

No response at first, then she said, "I don't think a reporter is someone to confide in."

He wanted to say, *How about the man you just kissed?* But instead he said, "I told you, anything you tell me will be off the record. It won't go any further."

Her cell phone rang. She shifted, slowing the car, and dug it out of her jacket pocket. She flipped it open, and from where he sat, Joe could see the voice-mail message flashing on the screen. She hit a button and got the screen of missed calls, and almost stopped in the middle of the road as she studied it. Then she flipped the phone shut and dropped it onto the console with a muttered, "Damn it all."

He wondered what was going on, why she wasn't on the phone immediately calling in for her voice mails.

As they entered the drenched town, the storm hadn't dampened the festivities. There were fewer people around, but tents were everywhere, and partiers darted back and forth, with huge umbrellas protecting them, going from shelter to shelter. He could hear the music that was still being pumped in. He checked the clock in the car dash. It was almost nine.

"It's still going on," she said softly.

"Come rain or sleet or snow or the dark of night," he murmured.

She sighed. "Do you feel as if this isn't part of the real world here, sometimes?"

"It's real," he said. "Just a different take on reality. I guess it's quite a change from what you're used to."

"Like night and day."

"So is it better or worse?"

She slowed the car as a group of people darted across the road, umbrellas bobbing over them. Then she drove slowly on toward the middle of the town and still hadn't answered him by the time she slipped her car into a parking slot by his truck. He didn't get out right away, and when she turned toward him, he said, "Well, what is it? Better or worse?"

She closed her eyes for a moment. "Worse, I think…no, I don't know."

He studied her for a long moment, the way tendrils of hair that had escaped from her ponytail started to curl from the moisture in the air and the way her lashes shadowed her eyes. "Why *are* you here?"

She bit her lip again, and he knew she was thinking hard. "I've told you—"

"I know what you've said, but it's obvious you aren't happy being here," he said bluntly. "You'd rather be working, rather be some other place in the world, but you're here. And you're miserable."

"I'm sorry about what happened back there." He didn't know if she meant the crying or the kissing or both.

"If you're apologizing, it's not necessary," he said softly. "I figure that whatever's going on with you, it has to be pretty important to you to come to the island and stay like this."

"It is," was all she said. If she'd been vulnerable before, she was closed-off now. "And there's your truck. Thanks for the dinner and…for everything."

He had the urge to take her hand in his, the hand curled into a tight fist on her lap, and hold it until he felt that tension seep away. "So that's it?"

She turned from him. "What more is there?"

He had a lot of ideas for what more there could be, but obviously she wasn't interested. "Nothing," he replied, and opened the door to the chilly night.

He hesitated with the door still open. He couldn't let it go. He thought she'd enjoyed the time with his family, and he knew damn well he'd enjoyed watching her smile and talk. No, he'd done more than enjoy it. Something had settled in his soul as he'd watched her. He looked at her, her face revealed now in the overhead lights. "The offer still stands if you want to talk off the record."

He didn't miss the way her eyes narrowed on him. "What about?" she asked.

"Anything," he said, and meant it.

"No comment," she said evenly.

He knew when he'd lost. "Okay, we'll stick to the interview and leave the rest of it alone."

"Good idea," she said.

"Listen," he said, wishing he really could just let it go and stick to business. But he couldn't. "I don't know you very well, but—"

"No, you don't know me," she said abruptly.

That shut him up and he climbed out and swung the door closed. Before he'd even grabbed the door handle on his truck, her car was backed up and on its way down the street. He turned and headed in two long strides up onto the walkway. He got out his keys and went into the office.

He didn't have to call out or look around to know he was alone in the building. Through the dim illumination of the security lights, he headed for his office cubicle. He stripped off his damp jacket, then sat in the chair behind his desk. He started to put in a call to his house, but hung up before touching a single number.

He'd been going to tell his mother he was staying at the office for the night, something he'd done every so often when he had a lot of work to do. But tonight was different. After what she'd said to him about Alegra, he knew if he said he was staying in town for the night, she'd put two and two together and come up with thirty-seven. She would assume he was finally getting a love life, and it began with Alegra.

You don't know me. Alegra had spoken the truth. He didn't know her. He wanted to know more and more about why she seemed so incredibly sad sometimes and why she could smile and literally light up his world other times.

He drew his hand away from the receiver and tipped back in the chair, clasping his hands behind his neck. Every encounter he had with Alegra only cemented an attraction he knew wasn't one-sided. Yet, it was an attraction that could, for him, be messy and wrong. Oh, he had no doubt that sleeping with her would be beyond anything he could imagine; he felt a tug of desire in his body just from the memory of the kiss. But what about when it ended? And it would have to end. She wasn't going to stay here, and he wasn't going to go anywhere, not as long as Alex needed to be on the island.

He sat forward, the front legs of the chair hitting the floor with a thud. The facts were pretty damn clear. And he'd never been a man who casually went in and out of relationships. For that moment, he almost wished he was like that—hit and run. Take what was there, then move on. That he could be close to Alegra, then watch her leave.

He went out into the main room and crossed to a small closet. He took out an extra jacket he kept there, then headed out into the rainy night. Joe had been alone for most of his life, by choice. He'd married Jean, by choice. They'd had Alex and they'd broken up, by choice. He'd never been pressured into anything. He'd made the choices that led to this point in his life. Good or bad, they were *his* choices. Now he chose to pull back from Alegra and the complications that would come with her.

Chapter Nine

Alegra awoke with a start to a window-rattling rendition of a John Philip Sousa march. She was on the couch, where she'd lain down, fully dressed, after coming back last night, and she'd obviously fallen asleep there. She sat up, rotating her neck to ease the kinks. The music changed to someone talking on a loudspeaker, encouraging people to enjoy their stay at "Old Bartholomew's celebration."

She stood and her cell phone clattered to the floor. Now she remembered using it to check her e-mail while she laid down, then nothing. She headed into the bathroom to shower and dress in fresh clothing. She didn't let herself recall the way she'd fallen apart in the car with Joe, or kissed him with mind-boggling desperation.

In half an hour she was back in the living area, opening her computer. Work blocked so much out, and she depended on that today. She realized she was almost grateful for the problem at their Boston store—an employee stealing and selling the products at ridiculously low prices on the Internet. It gave her a focus that lasted for most of the day.

She had her meals brought in, and except for an occasional need to stretch her legs, worked right through the day, even blocking out the sounds of the festival. She was just beginning to feel a degree of relaxation when she noticed the painting of the lighthouse, still propped by the door.

Without warning, the memories of the day before flooded over her, the child and the man, the time at the beach, then the Lawrence house. The dinner, the laughter and the conversation that had come so easily at that table. Then going to the car with Joe and rain making bubbles of the soap-writing on the windows.

She wasn't sure why she'd laughed so hard, or why that laughter had turned to tears and wrenching sadness. And then Joe reaching for her, kissing her, and her responding—it all seemed so very right. A connection that went beyond anything she'd ever had, and she'd let herself go with it. Until she realized it was a fantasy. The whole day was a fantasy, not reality. Not even close.

She sat back and pressed one hand to her mouth, as if the action would stop Joe's taste. It didn't. The moment Joe kissed her was a living thing for her, and she stood quickly, going to the small bar that had been neatly set into an old Victorian armoire. She didn't drink very much and she rarely drank alone, but she found a bottle of cognac, a snifter on a high shelf, and poured herself a shot. She moved to the couch, crossed her legs, and sipped, staring out through the windows at the coming night. No rain, just a cloudy sky.

Suddenly there was a soft knock on the door. She glanced at the clock. Seven already. She padded barefoot to the door and opened it.

"Joe."

Joe stood there, his denim jacket open to show a white, open-necked shirt underneath, worn with the faded jeans and boots. She couldn't deny her instant reaction—first surprise, then pleasure, then apprehension. The man seemed to fill the world around her, blurring out every other thing, and her first impulse was to slam the door shut and hide.

ALL DAY JOE had been walking around town, half expecting to see Alegra coming toward him. He'd prepared himself for that moment, when he met those amber eyes. He'd been bracing himself for it, but when he hadn't seen her anywhere, he'd felt let down. *You don't know me,* she'd said last night. And he didn't. But he *wanted* to know her.

That was when he'd had the idea to come to her cottage, walk up to the door and knock on it. Now he'd done that and she was right in front of him, and he was staring at her like some artless teenager. The lights from the room behind her made a halo of her loose hair. She wore a sweatshirt and jeans, and looked for all the world like a kid. Her amber eyes were regarding him intently.

"Why are you here?" she asked with a frown.

Just the sight of her was bringing a response he definitely didn't want at the moment. "I wanted to talk to you."

That brought a deeper frown. "I thought I told you I didn't want to talk."

"Nothing personal," he said quickly, but didn't mean it.

Her expression darkened even more, and it jarred him. There was something so familiar about the look. It came out of the past, way back when he was a kid, but he couldn't pin it down. Just then the heavens opened and the rain came in torrents.

Alegra stared at him, then finally said with more than a bit of grudging, "I guess you better come in." There wasn't any welcome in her invitation.

She moved back and he stepped over the threshold, closing the door behind him. Then he turned to face her, and met her eyes.

That was it! It was her eyes. The frown there. The unveiled expression in them that let him know she didn't want him here, but wasn't about to tell him to leave. The jolt of recognition seemed to come out of nowhere. A child looking so young and so unwelcoming superimposed over the image of the woman in front of him. The lighthouse. The huge rock. The girl sitting on that rock.

Everything fell into place, making a crazy sense for him. His mind raced as piece after piece fit into place. The girl he and his friends had stumbled on more than once sitting alone there, her legs bent, her head pressed to her knees. Just the way the woman Alegra sat there.

Farfetched as it seemed, he was beginning to think that Alegra Reynolds was that girl. The girl with amber eyes who had glared at anyone who intruded on her solitude. There had been whispers about that girl, about her mother disappearing and her father being a crazy drunk.

But Alegra had said she'd never been here before, that the island was a strange place for her. Then again, she'd found the parking clearing by the lighthouse. She'd been upset off and on, and he'd sensed she found no pleasure here.

One thing he knew for sure. He wasn't going to leave here until he knew the truth.

ALEGRA WAS UNNERVED by the way Joe was studying her, not saying a thing.

"I need to…" he finally started, pausing as if to find the right words, and all that did was make Alegra more tense.

Letting him in the cottage had been a mistake. Now he wanted to talk to her about something, and she prayed it would be something impersonal and brief.

Instead of giving her an answer, he tugged the front of his jacket open, as if getting the wetness of the back off him, and she did the polite thing. "Let me take that," she said.

Quickly, she put it on a peg by the door, then turned and found Joe looking around the room. His blue eyes skimmed over the expensive antiques, the plush rugs and the highly polished wooden floor. She could see him take in the desk, her papers, computer and the cell phone lying there. Then he turned back to her. Without thinking, she crossed her arms on her breasts and moved to let her hips rest back against the cool wood of the door.

"If I can wait here a bit, I'm sure the rain'll let up," he said.

His presence was diminishing her ability to breathe. "Do you need a ride?" she asked.

He crossed to the painting propped against the wall. He crouched in front of it and eased the brown paper back to expose it completely. She thought he'd say something like "It's a great painting" or "You really overpaid," but he didn't. He asked, "Why did you buy this particular painting?"

He cast her a look over his shoulder, and she found herself blinking at the intensity of his gaze. "Why not? It's very good, and I collect things I like."

"It is good," he murmured as he stood again. But he didn't turn to her. Instead, he crossed to the windows, looking out at the rain-drenched evening. "We're used to wet weather around here, but this is more rain than we've ever had for the festival."

He was making small talk, and she moved closer to him. She could see his reflection in the glass, blurred and almost surreal, partly from the streaking rain and partly from the lack of light. "That's why they should have it another time during the year," she said.

Before she could ask him again why he was here, he was the one asking a question. "So, you've never been here before?"

Something in the way he asked this made her tense. "Did I say that?"

He turned and she faced the reality of the man. It had been much easier to watch his reflection than to meet those deep blue eyes now. "I thought you did," he murmured.

Had she slipped up? She thought she'd just not said anything about it. But she said, "No, I never said that."

"So, you have been here before?"

She turned from him, caught a glimpse of her glass and the bottle of cognac on the table where she'd left them. She didn't hesitate crossing to them, sinking onto the couch and pouring more in her glass, ignoring the unsteadiness in her hands. "Help yourself," she said without looking at Joe. "There're glasses in the armoire."

He quietly crossed to the cabinet, then she heard the clink of glass on glass. He came back into her line of vision, sat in the chair across from her and reached for the bottle of cognac. He poured himself a little, then watched her so intently she couldn't keep meeting his eyes. So she moved back into the cushions, sat cross-legged and stared into her snifter.

He sipped some cognac, then said, "I'm here for the interview. I don't want to give up on it."

Rain beat on the glass, but Alegra didn't look away from Joe. "Why not? It's not going to get you a Pulitzer."

"I'm not looking for a Pulitzer," he countered.

"Well, I'm definitely not interesting enough to support any sort of story."

He shook his head. "You don't think so?"

She touched her upper lip with her tongue. "I don't think so."

"But you're here, and you came a long way to be here. How long are you staying?"

"Until after the ball."

She was getting more and more uncomfortable with this line of talk. He went on, "I could understand it if you'd been here before and wanted to come back, but to spend what it costs for the ball and do it on a whim?"

She finished what was in her glass, then put it on the table. When she looked at Joe again, she was hit hard by his expression. Waiting and expectant. She knew without question that he'd figured out who she really was.

She looked down at her hands clasped in her lap, seeing how white her knuckles were and feeling the bite of her nails in her palms. She didn't look at him when she spoke. "If I tell you anything personal, it can't go any further until I give my approval." She lifted her gaze to meet his and this time she didn't blink. "Agreed?"

He studied her, then finally said, "Agreed."

"Okay," she said, releasing a deep sigh. Her hands pressed to her knees and she tried to think how to start. Then she knew. She'd begin at the beginning. "I was born here." He didn't show any sign of surprise. She'd been right. He knew.

"There was never anyone named Alegra Reynolds living around here when I was growing up," he said. "The only Reynolds was Natty Reynolds, the original owner of the feed store, which is where Angelo now has his gallery." Joe took a sip of cognac, but his eyes never left hers over the rim of his snifter. "Natty died a bachelor and had no family."

He was leading to the inevitable truth, and something in her recognized the fact that he probably knew where it was going even before she started to talk. She shifted on the seat, clasping her now empty snifter between both hands, and pulling her elbows against her sides self-protectively. This was it. "I'm no relation to Natty Reynolds." He nodded slightly. "I took my grandmother's last name, but Alegra is my real first name." He stayed quiet, and she felt tension in her becoming almost unbearable.

She nodded. "Alegra Peterson. No one called me Alegra back then." She bit her lip, then said, "They called me Al, or little Al, or pitiful Al, or sad little Al."

The pain in her voice was just there and she couldn't do a thing about it. She didn't try to. At least she wasn't crying. "Al Peterson," he repeated. Then he took her totally by surprise by saying, "You used to sit on the rock under the lighthouse."

It was a statement, not a question, and it stunned her. "How did you know that? How did you recognize me? I don't look anything like I did as a kid."

He took another sip from his drink before answering her. "It's the eyes."

"Excuse me?"

"Your eyes, the look in them. I remembered that same look in your eyes back then."

This was crazy. "What look?"

He tossed off the last of his drink, but didn't make a move to refill it. "That look," he said, and motioned with his empty glass toward her. "The 'go away and leave me alone' look."

"I liked being alone at the rock," she said defensively.

"That's why you bought that painting?"

"I don't know." She really didn't, not anymore. There was no revenge buying the painting of Sean Payne. He'd never know she had his painting or care, for that matter. He'd have his money. And buying it just to remember the lighthouse didn't sit right with her, either. The moment she left the island, she'd probably put it away and forget about it.

"Why did you come back?" he asked bluntly.

"I came to tie up a loose end—a couple, actually, and after I do, I'm leaving and I won't be back. I'll stay out there in the real world."

"I thought this place was pretty damn real."

"It's not *my* reality. I don't want any part of it." She knew the harshness of her words jarred him, but she didn't try to soften them. "It's all yours."

He narrowed his gaze on her, but nothing lessened the intensity of his look. "You hate it here. Why?"

She hadn't planned on telling him anything else, but that single word cut into her, and she started talking, words tumbling out on words, telling him in a rush about her childhood, just bits and pieces, but she knew he was putting it all together. She tried to skim over how alone and miserable she'd been. And he'd seen her on the rock, without having a clue why she was there or what was going on with her. Her mother had walked out on her and her father and she had never heard from her or of her again.

She got to her father and his drinking, and the day she knew she was leaving. She got to the moment she stepped on the ferry, getting away from the father whose drunken rages were only increasing, and the islanders who taunted her or humiliated her with their charity and their pity.

She stopped, spent, and the only sound was that of the rain outside. Joe shifted, sitting forward and putting his glass on the table. "So you ran away?"

She nodded.

"Where did you go?"

She could tell him this much more easily than the other things. She told him about going to her grandmother's, getting the scholarship for college, then her big break with a very respected designer who, after seeing her designs, had agreed to mentor her.

JOE HAD NO IDEA what he'd helped to unleash until he listened to Alegra's torrent of words, which matched in intensity the storm outside. He ached at the pain he heard in them, and found himself in unknown territory with a woman—wanting to protect her from all the evil and pain in the world. Just as he did with Alex.

Gradually, her words slowed, and her tone got lower and less animated. By the time she waved a hand vaguely and said, "The rest, as they say, is history," her voice was barely above a whisper.

She stared down in her empty snifter and Joe watched her. Internally he couldn't begin to fathom what she'd felt back then. He sought words that wouldn't bring back the pain she'd just exposed to him to ask the main question of her. "Why did you come back at all?" he finally asked.

She sat forward, put her glass on the coffee table, then settled back into the cushions with a heavy sigh. She looked as if all emotion had been drained out of her. She didn't meet his gaze. "To wipe out the past."

He wanted to do that very thing for her, wipe out the things that little girl had endured, but he didn't know how anyone could do it for her. "How?" he asked.

She clasped her hands tightly in her lap. "I thought and thought about that over the years. Then three months ago a business associate started telling me about this place. He had no idea I'd ever been here. He talked about the festival and how he was quite certain the proceeds from it kept the island afloat, so to speak. And I got to thinking that maybe now, instead of *me* being the needy one, I could make this place need *me*."

He heard her words, but for the life of him, he didn't understand where she was going with this. "You mean, make them beg?"

That brought a smile, but there was no humor in the expression. It was almost a grimace. "Not that the concept doesn't hold a certain amount of appeal for me," she said, "but that isn't going to happen."

He stayed in his seat, never taking his eyes off her. "Then what *is* going to happen?"

She met his gaze then and spoke in an even tone. The passion of moments ago when she'd described her life here was gone. "I have money, lots of it, and I decided to make a donation to the island. A large one. I decided to come here and go to the ball, where I would be thanked publicly. You see, they asked on their paperwork when I sent in the donation if I would be willing to be thanked this way. I agreed, because it fit right in with what I've wanted to do for a long time." The smile was back, and this time he didn't like it at all. "What do you think those people will do when Alegra Reynolds steps up to be thanked for the staggering amount of money she's donated, and they find out that Alegra Reynolds is really Al Peterson? Because I'll tell them."

Now he understood and it brought a bitter taste to his tongue. "So that's it? All you came back for was to humiliate the townspeople and get your revenge?"

Chapter Ten

Alegra disliked Joe's take on her reasons for being here, but the next moment, she embraced it. It made it clearer for her. "You know, I think that's it. Humiliation and revenge. Sweet and neat." She sat forward and her voice was louder now. "And they'll take my money and they'll do what I tell them to do with it. Then I'm leaving, and this place can go to—" She cut off the curse before it came out. "This place won't exist for me any longer, and I'll be free."

He was looking at her with an expression she hated. Pity. "And you think that doing that validates everything you are and who you've become?"

She felt heat rise in her cheeks, and she got to her feet. "No, it won't. I'm valid, here or back in New York or San Francisco. I don't need that from any of the islanders."

"Then why this grandstanding? Why do you need it?"

She closed her eyes and shook her head. "You've got it all wrong."

"How do I have it wrong?" he asked.

Alegra felt exhausted. Once she'd started talking, she couldn't stop, and now that she *had* told Joe the truth, she wished she hadn't. For the pity and condemnation in his eyes made her stomach churn.

What had she expected after she'd bared her soul to him? A "Good for you. Throw it at them, then get back to your real life"? That hadn't come, and now all she felt was tired and defensive and off balance.

The rain beat on the cottage and she heard a low rumble in the distance. "It doesn't matter," she answered at last and knew she wanted him gone. Being alone was far better than being with a man who pitied her. She rose to her feet.

But he didn't move. "Why did you come back days before the ball if you wanted to just strike, then make your escape?"

He made it sound like war. "I had things to take care of, and I thought I'd need the extra time."

"Things?"

He wasn't letting it go. "Okay, my father's house. I wanted to take care of getting rid of the place. Either sell it or burn it to the ground, I don't give a damn. I just want it gone. There. Are you satisfied?" She'd heard the quaver in her voice and tried, in vain, to get control of herself. But soon she was shaking, and Joe must have noticed, because he stood and moved close to her.

He tipped his head to one side, his lashes lowering to hide some of his expression as he said softly, "Maybe you came back for something else."

"What?" she asked through clenched teeth.

"If you don't know, I surely don't," he said, then unexpectedly touched her cheek with his knuckles. His heat startled her as much as the contact and she realized how very cold she was right then. She moved her head, breaking the contact.

"I just told you why I came back," she muttered. "I can't help it if you don't approve."

"It's not up to me to approve or disapprove," he said.

She wrapped her arms around herself. "At least be honest and tell me that you don't approve, that you think I'm being petty or stupid or mean or egotistical."

"No, you're just being very human," he said in a low voice.

"And that's so bad?"

"In this context, it's empty. It's meaningless."

"I didn't tell you so you could judge me. It's not up to you to judge me on anything."

"Why did you tell me?"

God help her, she really did want his approval. She didn't even know why not having it made her feel so shattered and unfocused. "You asked. You pushed me."

"And you told me."

She hadn't told anyone else about her plans, except Roz, whom she'd instructed to send the committee running the ball a check, along with her approval to announce her name at the ceremony."

And now she'd explained everything to Joe. And he wasn't buying it, or at least, he wasn't liking it. "Maybe I thought you'd understand," she said with raw truth.

He touched her again, this time putting a finger

under her chin to bring her face up to his and not allow her to close him out by shutting her eyes. She didn't close her eyes.

"Oh, I think I do," he said.

Lightning flashed, bathing the room in harsh light, then thunder followed on its heels. She flinched. "I...I hate thunder," she whispered as lightning flashed through the room again.

She closed her eyes now and reverted to a childish coping mechanism. "One thousand one, one thousand two, one—" Thunder rolled.

"It's close," Joe said, obviously knowing what she was doing.

She was really shaking now, and couldn't do a thing to stop it. That was when Joe cupped the nape of her neck with his hand. "Thunder is just sound produced by rapidly expanding air along the path of the electrical discharge of lightning."

"Another definition," she said. His fingers wove into her hair, and she could feel him easing her closer to him. She didn't fight it. When thunder came again, she trembled, but this time the cause wasn't only the thunder.

She stared up at Joe, the simple act of breathing beyond her. Before she could figure out how to keep taking in air and letting it out, he lowered his head to find her parted lips with his.

She felt his lips, his heat, the hardness of his body against hers, and the world grew gray around the edges, narrowing more and more until the only reality was this contact with him.

Almost of their own volition, her arms lifted and slipped around his neck. She moved closer to him, felt his heat and strength as his arms closed around her. In the next heartbeat, she experienced the insane sense of coming back to something. He'd said she had more reasons to be here than what she'd told him. She would have sworn he'd been wrong, but now she wasn't so sure. It was very close to a feeling of home-coming, returning, but that made no sense; not any more than her next thought, that maybe he was the one she'd come back for.

Irrationally, that scared her, and she was going to push back. She was going to stop this. She was going to get away from Joe.

Instead, she did the opposite. When his tongue eased into her mouth, she opened herself to him. When he pulled her more tightly against him, letting her feel his desire for her, she didn't fight it. She didn't even think of fighting it. She got as close as she could, her fingers tangling in his damp hair, and the beginnings of a new beard bristled against her skin. His lips left hers, but didn't break their contact. They trailed to her throat, to a spot by her ear, and fireworks seemed to be everywhere.

She arched back, exposing her throat to him, letting him taste her flushed skin. She felt him tugging her sweatshirt up and off. She wasn't wearing a bra, and her nakedness was exposed. His hands were on her skin, and she heard a deep groan. It came from her, from her soul, and all the while the word *homecoming* was running through her mind. She moved frantically, not understanding the feelings, but knew she wanted to keep contact, and have more contact.

She tried to get his shirt up and out of the way. She pulled on it, heard buttons give, then the shirt was on the floor. She felt his heart beating under her palm, his slick heat against her, then she tasted him, skimming her tongue and lips across his hot skin. She brushed the suggestion of soft hair by his nipples, then the line of the same hair going down toward his flat stomach.

They were moving backward, at least she was, with Joe maneuvering her, and then she was on the couch, sitting. Joe was in front of her, dropping to his knees, pushing between her legs, and their eyes almost level with each other. Homecoming.

The fire in her was in him. She could see it burning in his gaze, then in the touch of his hands, framing her face. The kiss that came then was as urgent as any kiss in her life. It demanded things she couldn't begin to define. He pressed closer, his mouth dipping to the nakedness of her breasts. Then his lips were on her nipple, and the tightening in her grew until it was almost unbearable.

There was another groan as his mouth shifted to her other nipple. She pulled him closer, exploring him with her hands, and Joe did the same with both his hands and his lips. She arched toward him, feeling him between her legs, pressing his hardness against her, and she lifted her hips.

Homecoming. She had come home. And she had this, here and now. On the island. With this man. She knew she wasn't stopping. She knew she couldn't and accepted that fact with resignation and excitement.

JOE WANTED NOTHING MORE than to make love to her. The desire overwhelmed him. He felt her yielding to him, her softness under his hands, her taste in his mouth, and the idea of *not* going any further never entered his mind.

Until the world shifted on its axis. A disembodied voice announced clearly from somewhere in the room, "You have mail." It was just a voice, but it had the power to cut through him, and he stilled.

He looked down at Alegra under him on the couch, into her shadowed eyes heavy with desire, and it was all up to her. Either she ignored the voice and came to him, or she didn't. It was her choice. The voice came again, announcing "incoming mail," and when Alegra shifted to one side, away from him, he knew she'd made her choice.

Her getting to her feet was the equivalent of being doused by a bucket of cold water. The desire was still there—hell, he'd have to be blind not to see how sexy this woman was. But the common sense he'd used to change his life in the recent past came back full force. Sexy and desirable was one thing. Ruining a life he'd just started to rebuild by making the same mistakes he'd made with Jean was something else again.

He turned from her and the sight of her naked breasts as she reached for her sweatshirt. He didn't want to see her tightened nipples, the flush to her skin. He reached for his own shirt, shrugged it on, felt the nubs of thread where the buttons had been and left it open and loose.

He turned back to Alegra, who was standing by the desk now, staring down at her laptop, but not touching the keys. The sweatshirt was covering her, but he still had to fight the vivid memory of her taste and feel. "So you've got mail," he said.

She closed the computer and turned to him. A wall was up now, a barrier he didn't know how to get past, even if he wanted to right then. She didn't come closer as she spoke. "I'm sorry about…" She motioned vaguely around the room with her hands, then clasped them tightly together in front of her. "I mean, I shouldn't have…"

"I guess neither one of us should have," he said.

Color brightened her cheeks. "What I meant was, whatever I did, or whatever I said, or anything, I'm sorry."

He'd had apologies in his day, but this one was as nonspecific as any he'd ever heard. "Sure, that makes two of us."

Those amber eyes held his gaze, and although her lips might still look slightly swollen from the kisses, her mind was obviously back on why she was here in the first place. "Then I guess we're even."

"Yeah, and no story about your plans for…" He met her eyes directly and finished, "Whatever."

He saw her flinch. "Write whatever you want after I leave."

"Don't worry," he said. "I won't preempt your strike."

Color rose in her cheeks. "No, you don't understand at all."

Why did she make it sound as if he'd failed a huge, important test? He grabbed his coat off the chair and pulled it on, barely able to look at her now. "Thanks for the cognac," he said, and headed for the door.

Before he could get to the exit, Alegra said, "Joe?"

He turned, casting her a slanted glance. "What?"

She shook her head. "Nothing."

He opened the door and stepped out into the night. The rain had let up, but the mists and cold lingered on. He walked to his truck by the office and drove home. Some of his frustration and tension eased as simple reason came in to play.

If he had learned one thing in this life, it was that you don't change people. You can only change yourself, and he had no intention of doing that. Alegra hated this place. She was leaving as soon as she'd done what she'd come to do. She wouldn't look back. And he'd still be here. He'd still be doing his human-interest pieces and raising Alex and making a home.

Joe stepped into that home fifteen minutes later and made his way through the darkened rooms. He got to his bedroom when a voice came out of the darkness. "Joey?"

He turned and could barely make out his mother in the shadows at the end of the hallway. "Sorry, I didn't mean to wake you."

"You didn't. I was up." She came closer. "I was just starting to worry about your being gone so long." She was in a long blue bathrobe and holding a mug in her hand. "Is everything okay?"

"Fine, just fine."

"Good, good," she murmured. "You had a call while you were gone. It was Jean."

He felt his neck tense. "What did she want?"

"Seems she's flying to Japan and won't be able to get back in time for the holidays."

He relaxed. "We'll make out okay without her."

"I know we will, but Alex is going to ask questions."

She was right. His son seemed to have a knack for asking questions that had no answers. "I'll talk to him."

He was ready to go into his room when his mother asked another question. "Do you think Alegra could come to dinner tomorrow evening?"

He shook his head. "No. She's got work." He shrugged. "Nothing gets in the way of that."

His mother clicked her tongue softly. "Oh, Joey, we all have to work."

"Yeah, sure. Tell Alex that the next time he asks for his mother."

"That's different. Jean loves *only* her work." She paused, then, "I'm sorry. I didn't mean that she never loved you or Alex."

"She loves Alex in her own way." Loving him didn't matter to him, because he knew now he'd never loved her. "But she's made her priorities."

"Yes, she has. But don't you think Alegra is different? She seems so vulnerable, so…" She sighed. "I don't know, lonely, don't you think?"

Yes, he did. "You're probably right, but it's not our business."

"Isn't it?"

"Mom, just because she broke bread with us… It doesn't mean anything except she was hungry."

His mother patted his arm, said, "Good night," then

headed down the hallway to the room she shared with his father.

He went into his own room, closed the door, and without turning on any light, stripped out of all of his clothes except his briefs, then got under the covers. He welcomed the feel of the cool sheets against his skin. Rolling onto his side, he looked out the window and saw a hazy moon just showing itself in the blackness of the sky. He closed his eyes, but opened them immediately when an image of Alegra, naked, came to him with stunning brilliance. His body responded instantly.

He groaned and slipped out of bed, then padded to the bathroom, and stripped off his underwear. He turned on the shower, then stepped under the spray before it got warm. While the outward response of his body ceased, the images in his mind of what had happened with Alegra earlier did not. He uttered a curse that didn't banish Alegra any more than the water did, and he faced the fact that when it came to women, he made bad choices. Very bad choices. But he was determined to stop that pattern right now, right here.

He awoke hours later in the early-morning light. The sky through the window was clear for once, no rain. Alex was curled up in bed with him. He vaguely remembered the boy coming into his room, saying he had a bad dream, and climbing under the covers with him. He raised himself on one elbow and looked down at his son. His fair hair was tousled from sleep, and his improbably long lashes lay curving against his smooth skin. Joe was looking at the very reason he was not going to repeat the past. Alex was everything to him, and the driving force behind changes Joe had made in his life. He wasn't going to blow it all now.

He eased out of bed and pulled on his jeans, then carried the cordless phone on the nightstand into the bathroom and closed the door. He called information, got the number, then called the Snug Harbor Bed and Breakfast. It was answered on the second ring by someone who seemed awfully damned cheerful for such an early call.

"The Snug Harbor, good morning."

"Connect me to Ms. Reynolds's cottage."

"Sorry. She's not here."

Joe's hand tightened on the receiver. "Okay, I'll call back later."

"Sir, she left. She won't be back, at least not today."

"What do you mean, she left?"

"She called last night, asked for the ferry schedule and said she was leaving on the first ferry this morning," the woman said.

He closed his eyes, stunned that Alegra had just walked away. He'd thought her passion for revenge would have at least kept her here, but something in him lifted to hear that she'd given up that notion.

"So she just left?"

"About an hour ago."

"Thanks," he murmured and would have hung up, but the woman spoke again.

"You can leave a message if you like."

"I can?"

"She left, but she kept the cottage. She said she'll be back for one night." She named a date, and he recognized it as the night of the ball. She wasn't going to walk away from her moment of glory, after all. His heart sank. "So I can give her a message when she returns."

"No message," he murmured, and hung up.

He stood there, his back against the cold wood of the door for a long moment. She'd left. She was gone, but she'd be back to do what she came here for in the first place. A knot settled in his stomach. Revenge would be hers.

He'd called to tell her that he was going to be really busy with things for the rest of her time here, and to wish her well. He'd had no intention of trying to talk her out of her plans. Now she was gone, and the decision was taken out of his hands. He wouldn't see her again. He certainly wasn't going to the ball. Funny how that left him with a peculiar emptiness.

"Daddy?" Alex called. Joe heard a knock on the bathroom door. "Daddy. I gotta go."

Joe opened the door and his son scooted past him. He waited, and when the boy was hitching up his pajama bottoms, Joe crouched down in front of him. "What are you doing today?" he asked.

Alex grinned. "Mamaw's gonna take us to see the pirate!"

He knew what the boy was talking about. There was a reenactment of Bartholomew's homecomings from his raids, and now that the weather had cleared, it would go ahead as planned. Down on the beach, there'd be men in costume, people watching and cheering as a series of dinghies brought the "crew" to the shore with their bounty, and the cannon would be fired at imaginary enemies out in the sound.

"Sounds like fun," he said, ruffling his son's silky hair.

"You coming?" the boy asked.

He nodded. "Sure, I'd love to come."

"Great!" Alex squealed and ran past his dad, disappearing through the bedroom and out into the hallway. "Mamaw! Mamaw!" he called out to his grandmother.

Joe stood, caught his reflection in the mirror of the pedestal sink and winced. He looked like a mile of bad road, from the spiked hair, to the shadow of a beard and the dark smudges under his eyes. She was gone. He exhaled and crossed to the sink to shave. She was gone. "Just in time," he said to himself, but the man facing him in the mirror didn't nod in agreement. His frown just deepened.

Chapter Eleven

Alegra watched the ferry chug off into the mist over the sound and didn't move until it was gone, lost from sight. Before she'd set foot on the island a few days ago, she'd been a woman of certainty who made decisions based on facts, who did not act on impulse. But all that had changed. She sank back in the car seat. She'd decided to leave the island on impulse, right after Joe had left her alone last night. She'd planned to get out of here and only come back for the ball, then leave again for good.

And yet, she'd pulled out of the lineup for the ferry and parked by the coffee stand. She'd watched the boat leave the dock, and then almost desperately wanted to be on it heading to the mainland. But reason had won out. Running away because she was unnerved and un-settled by the island, and the man she'd met on the island, was impulsive and unthinking.

She hit the steering wheel with the flat of her hand and muttered an oath, which did little to release her frustration. She reached for her cell phone and put in a call to Roz. The woman had been awakened in the early hours of the morning to be told about Alegra's changed plans. Now she was calmly listening to her boss tell her to forget what she said, that the original plans were back in place. Good assistant that she was, she didn't ask any questions.

Alegra hung up and wished she was as calm as Roz sounded. She turned the car to head back up the road to the highway, taking deep, even breaths, trying to get past her stupid actions of the morning. She wouldn't run. She'd stick to her plans. She'd finish this and leave. That became her mantra.

She got back into Shelter Bay and went directly to the Snug Harbor B&B, checked back in, then went to her cottage. As she sat in front of her computer, waiting for it to boot up, she glanced out the window and she saw a pale blue sky brushed with drifting clouds, saw the trees on the bluff sway in a light breeze. The island weather was as unpredictable as she'd obviously become. She settled in to work, blocking out the not-too-distant sounds of music and celebration. Hours later she was startled by the boom of a cannon. She pushed back from the desk. It was almost dusk now, and the only time she'd taken a break all day was when the girl from the main house had brought her a lunch tray. When she'd opened the door, she'd caught a glimpse of the street, with streams of people going up and down the way.

She stretched her hands over her head and thought she'd need a vacation after all this. That brought a chuckle. Sure, she'd take time off, maybe go to the Bahamas or

Hawaii or even Paris, and she'd take her computer and her cell phone with her and keep in touch and work. That was her life and right now it felt terribly empty.

Quickly she tried to push that thought away, along with the memory of Joe saying she needed a break, needed to turn off her cell phone for a while. But she failed. She'd managed to keep Joe and all thoughts of last evening out of her mind until this moment. She was good at compartmentalizing her thoughts, and Joe had been in a compartment she'd intended never to open again. The thing was, it opened on its own, and she was having trouble closing it again. She was having trouble forgetting how his kiss, his touch, his body had stirred her to a passion she'd never known before, and how she'd felt as if she'd come home.

A knock came at the door, and she was grateful for the distraction. Until she remembered that Joe had been at her door last night. Was it him now? She hesitated, then called out, "Who is it?"

"Just me, ma'am, Melinda. I've come to get your dishes and take your order for dinner if you want it in your cottage."

She opened the door to the same girl who'd brought her lunch. "Thanks," she said, handing the tray to the girl. "And yes, I would like dinner in the cottage. Some broiled chicken and lots of vegetables. Can you bring it in a couple of hours? I'll be hungry by then."

"Fine." The girl hesitated. "Oh, I thought I should warn you that they're going to be shooting off the cannon, so don't be alarmed by the noise."

"I heard it once already."

"Well, it's going to start up again soon." The girl smiled. "It know it sounds corny, but it's really fun. You should go down to see it, or take a look from the bluff. It's going on just down the beach from here."

"I'm pretty busy," Alegra said, not very excited by the idea of watching cannons being fired to mimic pirates sinking ships that came too close to the island. "But thanks," she said, and jumped when a booming sound shattered the air around her.

"The cannon," the girl said unnecessarily.

"The cannon," Alegra echoed, and closed the door.

She crossed to the window and looked out at the night. Past the wind-twisted pines clustered at the top of the bluffs, she saw flashing lights and could hear voices drifting on the cold air. The sounds of a brass band started up again, this time playing "A Pirate's Life." She shook her head. Leave it to this place to admire a pirate.

She turned from the view as a cannon on the beach thundered again. Despite the fact she knew what it was and where it came from, the sound still jarred her nerves. Joe hadn't been entirely right about the definition of thunder. He should have added "cannons when they're being fired." The moment she thought about Joe, she felt the emptiness again.

Another boom of the cannon, followed by more cheering and music, and she decided she had nothing to lose by going to the bluff and watching.

In minutes she'd reached the low metal railing that blocked any unintentional descent to the beach below.

She looked down and saw fire pits dug in the sand in a rough circle near the water. The flames danced into the air, casting a flickering glow over the bystanders, who all kept a respectful distance from the cannon itself, which had been set up right at the water's edge. She watched as a man with a torch approached the cannon and held the torch to the wick at the back of it. A sizzling sound and sparkling effect followed, and people moved farther back, most of them covering their ears, children and adults alike. Then the boom, and a cannonball shot from the barrel.

A cheer went up. The speakers began playing "They sailed their ship cross the ocean blue, bloodthirsty men and old Bartholomew," and spectators sang along. She remembered singing the same song in school, but back then the festival was nothing like this. Back then it was relatively simple, unlike the full Hollywood production it was now. Costumes everywhere, special effects, a row of old dinghies on the tide line…

She started to turn away when she caught a glimpse that stopped her. Joe. He was near the water, the flicker from the fire touching his face as he sang with the others. Alex was on his shoulders clapping with enthusiasm, and she thought she could see Joe's parents just behind.

"'Listen to our dark, dark tale as it's told, about the search for treasure and the lust for gold.'"

She saw Joe grin as Alex leaned down to say something to him. They both laughed, then some people started dancing near the cannon. The music changed back to "A Pirate's Life," and a man dressed in a costume broke into a jig by the cannon.

Debauchery, she thought in amusement, and couldn't quite understand why even a tiny bit of her, an obviously irrational part of her, wished she was down there. Without warning, Joe looked up in her direction and stopped singing. He couldn't see her, surely. It was too dark. He was too far away. But that didn't stop her feeling his eyes on her, then there was a smile, a slight nod, and she moved back quickly out of sight. Did the man have such good night vision?

"Damn it," she muttered, turning to head back to the cottage. When she went inside, she closed the door to shut out the festival, then was startled by the ring of her cell phone. She crossed to the desk to get it, and flipped it open. "Roz?"

"I left you four messages," her assistant said without preamble.

She'd left her phone here while she'd been outside, and four messages in that short absence didn't bode well for the rest of the evening. "What's going on?"

"It's James Ota. He's been calling every ten minutes. He's demanding that I give him your cell number or get a message to you right away."

Ota was the regional rep for her stores in the northeast. The man was good at what he did, but he saw even the most minor problems as a crisis. She sighed. Oh, well, she thought, right now she could use the diversion. "What's his problem?"

But it didn't turn out to be much of a diversion. For almost half an hour, Alegra listened to Roz tell her about a shipping mix-up and Ota's problems with a supplier.

She heard the words, knew what they meant, but she couldn't stop hearing the sounds coming from the beach below, couldn't stop imagining Joe and Alex in the midst of the celebration. She crossed to the windows with the phone pressed to her ear, and tugged the curtains across to block out the view. But it didn't block out the sound of the cannon being shot again.

"Good heavens," Roz said in her ear. "What was *that?*"

"Cannon fire," Alegra said.

"What?"

"Never mind," she said, turning her back on the windows.

She still found herself wondering what it would be like to be down there laughing, singing and enjoying the festivities. Then she flinched as another thought corrected the first one. It wasn't just being there, it was being there with Joe, and even Alex. Then she laughed. The idea was absurd. Alegra Reynolds down on the beach with an islander, and that islander's three-year-old?

"What's so funny?" Roz demanded.

"Oh, sorry. Just…" She exhaled. "Listen, tell James that he can hunt down Morris in New Jersey and have him figure out where the shipments are. I'm busy."

Roz was quiet for a moment, then, "Sure, okay. I'll do that. When can I expect you back in New York?"

"I don't know," she said. "I've got to finish up here, then…" Her words trailed off when she realized she wasn't sure any longer what she was going to do when she left. "I'll let you know."

"I put the instructions for what's to be done with the money you're donating in with the check."

"Thanks. It's an old lighthouse on the island that's not in working order and should be. I want all that money to be designated for its repair and upkeep, with the stipulation it's really running, not just a tourist destination."

After she hung up, Alegra closed the phone, then reopened it. She stared at the tiny screen with its color and various alerts. She took a deep breath, then pressed the end button, holding it down until the screen went blank. The phone was shut off.

She barely believed what she'd done, yet strangely she didn't have any urge to turn it back on. She tossed it onto the couch cushions, crossed to her laptop to shut it off, ignoring that blasted voice telling her, "You've got mail." The whirring of the disk drive stopped, and she closed the top. With that all done, she stood in the empty room, waiting for something. She didn't know what. A bolt of lightning? A voice from above telling her to turn the phone and laptop back on right now? Finally, all that happened was a wave of tiredness that washed over her so heavily she felt her legs start to shake.

She turned off the lights and went into the bedroom, stripped off her clothes and crawled into bed. She curled up on her side under the lavender-scented sheets and blankets, closed her eyes and, despite years of having trouble getting to sleep, barely had time to exhale before sleep overtook her. The sleep was deep and luxurious at first, but later became tense as she was gripped by a dream….

She was eight years old. She was by the water. It was cold, so very cold. Then she was sitting on the rock, her back to the bluffs, in her spot, closing her eyes.

"Alegra?"

Her name came to her on the night air. She opened her eyes to the flicker from fire rings under a dark, starless sky. And Joe. He was coming toward her, Joe the man, not Joe the boy, waving to her, jumping up onto the rock—and she wasn't eight anymore. She was a woman, reaching out, knowing that this was why she'd come to the rock. She felt his hand close around hers, heat replacing all the coldness in her world, and she let him pull her up and into his chest.

She let him hold her, let the thoughts of homecoming and being safe filter into her soul. When she lifted her face to kiss him, the contact was fierce, needy. His hands were on her, and the location shifted from the rock to softness all around. Lavender was everywhere, and warmth and gentleness. She fell into it, wishing it would go on forever, his naked body against hers. She arched toward him, and his whisper surrounded her. "Welcome home."

Her heart hammered. She clutched at him, holding on to him as if her life depended on it. She was home. She was home. It rang in her mind, over and over again, and he came to her, touched her, then entered her. Home.

"Ms. Reynolds! Ms. Reynolds!" A banging. A voice calling to her. Cutting through the dream. Robbing her of the dream. Joe was going, the images dissolving, and the heat went with him.

In one heartwrenching moment, everything changed.

Alegra was alone in the bed, pushing herself up, swiping at her tangled hair. Her body ached, and she was alone. "Welcome home." Joe's voice still lingered, and she shuddered at how much she wished she *was* home. That she was welcome and that Joe would be there.

Alegra made her way to the door and opened it to see Melinda.

"What do you want?" she demanded rudely.

The girl cringed back a bit. "Ma'am, your dinner."

"I don't want it."

She would have slammed the door right then, but the girl kept talking. "But a lady, Roz, she called and she's worried about you. You weren't answering your phone or—"

"I turned it off. I did that because I wanted some peace and quiet. If I don't answer the door, I don't want to be interrupted. Do you understand?"

"Oh, yes, ma'am, I'm so sorry," Melinda said quickly and scurried away with the tray in her hands.

Even during the confrontation, Alegra knew she was out of line. Raw nerves drove her, and when the girl left, she knew she'd have to apologize. She never spoke like that to her own employees.

Alegra returned to bed, and tossed and turned for the remainder of the night.

ALEGRA DRAGGED HERSELF out of bed at dawn, went into the living area, turned on her cell phone and the computer, then walked away from both of them. She had a shower, got dressed in corduroy slacks and a heavy-knit tunic, and pushed her feet into her boots. Without taking anything with her but her room key, she stepped outside into the chill morning. Like yesterday, clear blue skies.

She heard the sounds of the people at the festival, the music that seemed to always be piped into the air, and smelled the heavy scent of barbecue. It was the day before the ball, and there was always a huge cookout on the beach where the cannon had been fired. It was a pit barbecue, with music and games for the kids. Tomorrow was the parade, then the ball to finish the festival.

She'd never gone to the barbecue when she'd been a kid, and she didn't intend to go now. She had an apology to make and she headed for the main house. Stepping into the warmth of the huge Victorian, she saw Melinda coming down a hallway that led to rooms at the back of the house. She called out to her. "Melinda! Hello!"

The girl flushed slightly at the sight of Alegra coming toward her. She hugged a stack of clean towels to her chest. "Oh, ma'am, I really am sorry about last night, but I thought you wanted dinner. I never should have persisted, but the lady called and she was so insistent about getting a hold of you, too, and I—"

Alegra cut her off. "No, I came to apologize to you. I had no right to be so rude, and I'm very sorry. I do appreciate what you did."

"Thank you, ma'am," she murmured.

"What size do you wear?" Alegra asked.

The girl looked totally confused now. "Excuse me, ma'am?"

"Your size," Alegra repeated, eyeing her. "A ten?"

"Uh, yes, ma'am."

"Your favorite color?"

"Uh, I guess lavender."

"Great. I'll have something sent to you."

Melinda looked confused. "You will?"

"Yes, a gift, from me to you, to apologize." Before the girl could protest, Alegra said, "Please, I want to."

"Then thank you, Ms. Reynolds," she said, then color touched her cheeks. "I mean, not something too…well, you know."

Yes, she knew. "Of course. Nothing too racy."

The girl looked a little happier. "Do you need anything else, ma'am?"

"No, thanks, nothing," Alegra said.

The girl moved off and Alegra returned to her cottage. She called Roz to apologize to her, also. Her assistant took it all in stride, saying, "Pressure. I know how it is. Don't worry."

Pressure? Alegra guessed that was some of it. That and the fact that she still couldn't get her response to Joe in the dream—or in real life—out of her head. She told Roz to pick out something "spectacular but modest" in lavender and have it overnighted to the Snug Harbor B&B for Melinda.

After she hung up, she faced the day in front of her. She could spend it working, or she could spend it doing something she should have done the right way the first time. She went back out, climbed in her car and drove out of the lot.

It took her forever to get a few blocks down the street because of the throngs of people at the festival. When she finally broke free of them, she headed south to the gray, faded house with its brambles and weeds and the mustiness of age and abandonment everywhere.

She parked by the sagging steps of the porch and got out. The sunlight was very unkind to the house, exposing every warped board and dirty window.

The porch steps protested loudly as she moved up them and crossed to the door. It was then she realized she didn't even have a key with her. But before, when she'd been here, there'd been a key outside. She bent down and picked up a rusty old lawn ornament by the door. It hadn't stood up to time any better than the house had. But the extra key was still under it. She retrieved the key and opened the door. It swung back on creaking hinges.

She was looking into the house she'd walked away from ten years ago, the same furniture, heavy with dust. Mustiness hung in the fetid air. She made herself take one step in, then another, until she was all the way inside, standing in the small living room.

She never thought she'd do this again, but here she was. Home. Such as it was. She wandered through the four small rooms. The kitchen was filthy, and stained pots were still sitting on the small, grease-caked stove. The table held the ever present ashtray, filled to the brim with dried-out butts.

It was obvious that when her dad had died, the door had been locked and no one had ever come back. She glanced quickly at the counters, at the old appliances, the daisy-patterned canister set that was supposed to look happy and light, but only looked dreary and dull. She went into the short hallway, glanced into her father's old room, and saw the bed had been stripped. The linens were in a pile on the floor. His boots still lay on their sides at the foot of the iron-framed bed.

She didn't go in. She went to the only other bedroom in the house. Hers. She hesitated at the closed door, then reached out and opened it. From the hallway she saw her bed, made the way she had left it. Her dresser had nothing on it at all. She'd taken whatever she'd had there. The rug on the floor was heavy with dust. A small desk she used by the curtainless window had a lamp on it and a pencil. Beside it was a single slip of paper.

That was what drew her in. That got her to the desk. She knew what it was: the note she'd written so carefully before she'd slipped out before dawn and left her father passed out after a drunken binge in his room.

Dad: I'm going away. I don't belong here and I don't want to stay any longer. I will go to Grandma Elaine's. She said I could. I'll never be back. Alegra.

As she stared at the perfectly scripted words, she felt a pain so intense that she blindly reached for the bed and sank onto the edge of the mattress.

She clutched her middle and tried to breathe. She wasn't sure how long she sat there, but she finally stood and went back through the house to the front door. She stepped out, closed the door tightly behind her and just stood on the porch. She'd have someone come in, clean the place right out, paint it and make it decent, then put it up for sale. She didn't even bother to lock it.

Instead of going to her car she walked around behind the house, through the knee-high growth of weed-strewn grass and back into the woods. The ground under her feet was spongy with layers of leaves and needles, and although she couldn't see the path she used to take, she knew the way. And for a long time, she walked as she had as a child, past old haunts and down to the beach.

She didn't go near the lighthouse this time, only stared out at the water for a few minutes. She wasn't a teenager anymore, and nothing was the same. Just as she was no longer the same. That little girl was no more, even if the pain had survived.

As she headed back, she thought how her pain would soon be gone. She'd make sure it disappeared tomorrow night at the ball and never returned. When she rounded the corner of the porch, she saw the front door was ajar. Had she left it that way? No. She looked around, saw nothing. She listened, heard nothing. Then she went up the porch stairs and stepped into the house.

"Hello?" she called out, staying by the front door.

She heard a rustling sound, then footsteps and suddenly Joe emerged through the doorway that led to the hallway and bedrooms. The sight of him in her old living room made her feel invaded somehow. Her privacy stolen. And she'd left that note in her bedroom, she remembered now. Stupid. How could she have neglected to pick it up and destroy it? Stupid.

Chapter Twelve

"What are you doing in here?" Alegra demanded.

He looked too large for the small place, the bulky denim jacket and heavy boots only adding to the impression of size. He didn't respond to her question, said only, "They told me you'd left the island."

She stepped a bit closer, wishing she could just grab the man and pull him physically out of the house. "Obviously I didn't," she said, then repeated her original question. "What were you doing in there?"

"I saw the car outside. It surprised me, and I wondered if it was your car, or if someone else was here."

"So, you just came in and—?"

"I knocked. I called out, and no one answered, so I thought I'd better check to make sure everything was okay."

Logical and reasonable, but his answer made her tremble. Had he seen the note? She crossed her arms over her breasts. "Everything's just fine," she said, feeling the breadth of the lie as she uttered it.

"Good," he said, still not making any effort to leave, much to Alegra's displeasure.

"Why are you here at all?" she asked.

His gaze swept around the musty, neglected space. "Boyd told me where you used to live, and you'd mentioned being here on the island to sell the place." Of course, Boyd would know, she thought, but didn't say it. Joe moved closer, so close she could see the fine lines that fanned from the corners of his incredibly blue eyes. "I just wanted to take a look."

She stared at him. "Why?"

He studied her intently for so long that she felt she'd never take another breath. Then he said simply, "I thought it would help me understand."

She dropped her gaze to the front of his jacket, to the exposed *V* of his throat and the steady pulse beating there. "There's nothing here to understand," she whispered.

He reached out and touched her then, a light contact of fingertips on her shoulder she could barely feel through her jacket. "*You're* here."

She shook her head. "I shouldn't be."

She felt the sting of tears and fought crying with every fiber of her being. The last thing she wanted to do, here, now, with Joe present, was cry again.

She abruptly pushed past him, going into the hallway, then down to her old bedroom. She grabbed the note that lay where she'd left it, and in a frenzy, tore it into tiny bits. She crushed the pieces in her fist before going back out to the living room. Joe was still there. She ducked past him, heading to the door, then stepped out into the clear, cold day. Joe followed, and as soon as he was out she closed the door with a jarring slam and locked it, put the key under the lawn ornament, then turned and ran down the steps. Joe caught up to her at her car.

"Alegra?"

She stopped, pressing the fist with the pieces of the crushed note still in it on the hood of the car. She closed her eyes with her back to the man. "What?"

"Why didn't you leave? The bed-and-breakfast said you had."

She meant to shrug, but ended up shuddering instead. "Damn it," she muttered in a choked voice.

Joe was right behind her, his voice a low whisper. "And why are you here at the house when you said you'd never be back?"

So he'd read the note, and in a burst of frustration, embarrassment and fury, she spun around. She opened her fist, and the pieces of the note flew into the air and she swung at him with the flat of her hand as hard as she could. He grabbed her wrist, stopping her in mid-swing. "You had no right!" she screamed. "You had no right at all!"

He still held her wrist, and those blue eyes burned into hers. "It was just there, open, and I couldn't help but read it."

"Damn you," she said through clenched teeth, and her shudder came full force.

He pulled her to him, hugging her, and she fought being in his arms, pummeling his chest, his shoulders, and then around on his back. "Let it go, Alegra," he said, his words muffled by her hair. "Just let it go."

As JOE SPOKE, he felt her blows, but the fury in them decreased. He held her, letting her bury her face in his jacket and taking whatever blows she still had in her. He'd come here to understand her, that was true. And after he read the note, he understood so much more. He'd felt the pain of the child who'd written those words all those years ago. He had literally ached for her. Then she'd appeared, upset by his presence, yet haloed by a lingering sadness.

He'd have given anything to take away that sadness, to make her smile. Now she was in his arms. He could feel her heart pounding and each ragged breath she took. Her hands had stilled, the denim of his jacket balled in them, and he just held her. He let her take whatever she could from his embrace and prayed it was enough for her right now.

She finally pushed against his chest, trying to put space between them. The last thing he wanted to do was let her go. His eyes met her overly brilliant amber ones and he was rocked with the realization that you never chose the person you loved. That love chose *you*. And he was so very close to loving Alegra. The child she once was and the woman she'd become.

Still, he broke the contact, let her take a step back and press her open hand to the hood of her car behind her. He wanted to stroke her cheek, feel the silkiness of her skin. But he made no move. "I didn't deliberately read that note," he heard himself say. "I'm sorry."

Her tongue touched her lips quickly, then she gave a soft sigh. "It's not important."

It was damn important! he thought. He was about to say so, but as she turned, her legs seemed to buckle. He reached out, grabbed her arm and steadied her. "Let me drive you back," he said.

She must have felt really weak for she just nodded and let him lead her around to the passenger side of the car. He climbed in behind the wheel and found the keys in the ignition. With a glance at Alegra, who was fumbling to do up her seat belt, he started the car and drove her away from the old house.

When he got to the main road, he turned away from the town. As Alegra released a heavy sigh, he didn't think twice about reaching out and covering the hand clenched on her thigh with his.

She surprised him by turning the hand over and lacing her fingers with his, and then held on tightly as he drove. When the lighthouse came into view, he slowed, then turned into the deserted parking area.

He stopped near the bluffs, by the fence that protected the lighthouse from trespassers, and let the engine idle. To turn off the ignition, he'd have had to let go of Alegra, and he didn't want to do that. They sat that way for long minutes, and when he finally looked at her, she was staring straight ahead at the view of the sound. He could see a pulse beating wildly just under her ear, and her teeth were nibbling her bottom lip.

"You need to let it go, Alegra," he said. "Can you?"

There was no response at first, then one came he didn't want. She slipped her hand out of his, turned to the side window and said, "I will."

"When?" He already knew what her answer would be.

She didn't disappoint him. "After the ball," she whispered, turning to face him. She looked so *haunted*.

"Alegra," he said, switching off the ignition and resting his hand on the rich leather of her seat back, "do you really think humiliating the town and throwing money at them will heal all of this?"

She blinked. "It might."

"And if it doesn't?"

She shrugged. "I don't know."

He let himself touch her shoulder and he felt the unsteadiness in her. "Then what's the point of all this?"

She shook her head. "I just need to do it," she said. "I need to try."

He studied her. It was her plan, and she wasn't giving it up. She'd do it, then go back to her work. To the life she had. To the life she wanted. That put it in perspective for him, and he turned from her, ready to restart the car and get out of there. He'd take her back to her place, then go off and examine how this woman had managed to touch his soul, this woman whose wants and needs were so different from his.

"What's wrong?" she asked.

He looked back at her, and the strong sunlight coming through the windows etched the beauty of her face so strongly in front of him that he could barely stand looking at her. It only emphasized the way she'd snuck into his heart and his life. "What difference does it make what the people here think of you?"

She frowned at him. "I just want them to know they were wrong."

"Wrong to feel sorry for you, to care about what happened to you?"

She shook her head. "They didn't care. They just felt sorry for me and pitied me. There's a huge difference."

"How do you know if they cared or not?"

"I knew. I saw their looks and heard their whispers. I knew what they were saying, that the Peterson kid was pitiful, that she was just like her old man, a big nothing."

He cringed at her words. "You thought that?"

He could see her jaw clench. "I *knew* that."

"How? Are you a mind reader?"

The tension in her was increasing. "I didn't have to read anyone's mind. They *told* me what they thought of me."

"What are you talking about?"

She took a shuddering breath. "It was the Bounty Festival, and my dad brought home a pirate costume. I didn't know where he got it, just that there were boots, a billowy shirt and a hat. The stuff was a little big, but I had a costume and I could go to the festival." Her voice got lower. "So I did, and I went into town and there was this kid, Sean Payne." She was staring at her hands in her lap now. "The great artist. Back then he was just a bully. And he saw me and he laughed and said the costume was one his dad had thrown in the Dumpster by his office—which was by the bar my dad hung out at."

He waited, heard her take another shuddering breath,

and then, "He said I was a garbage pirate or something like that. The other kids with him were laughing and it was horrible. I…I went all the way to the lighthouse and threw the whole damn costume in the water, and I never went to the festival again—until now."

"God, I'm so sorry," Joe said.

"Sure, now you are, but back then, you would've been laughing and pointing, too. Your dad—he thought he was helping by stepping in, and he was kind, but I know he did it out of pity. You were probably there, too. You and the others."

His dad was a peacemaker, not a pitier. He wanted to tell her that, but knew that now wasn't the time to do that. And he *hadn't* been there, not that he remembered, and he wished he could've told her he never would've laughed at the fun Sean was having at her expense. But somehow he couldn't. All he could say with total truth was, "I'm sorry it happened to you, really sorry, but why do you think handing that check over will change things?"

"It *will* change things for me." She bit her lip. "I want to just do it, let them know that the little kid they used to find so pitiful is the one who's handing them enough money to…" She didn't bother to finish her sentence.

"And after you do it?"

"I'm out of here. I'm so far out of here that this island, these islanders, won't exist for me anymore."

But she'd exist for *him.* He knew that with painful certainty. He shifted to bring his hand up to cup the nape of her neck. He felt her heat, knew a powerful need for her. It made no real sense, beyond the fact that she was physically beautiful. But his response to her went so far beyond that, he couldn't begin to define it.

He would have drawn her closer, but she pushed his hand away. "Don't," she said and he drew back. "I don't need you to console me. I don't want your damn pity, too."

Pity had nothing to do with what he was feeling, but he didn't argue. Instead, all he said was, "You're no mind reader," then put the car in gear and backed out onto the road.

He took her into town, got her to the Snug Harbor, parked her car by the front building and got out. He left her there in the parking lot, knowing whatever could have happened, wouldn't. He couldn't help her, and she didn't want anything he could offer her. This was the end of a madness that had begun when he'd first spotted her on the ferry. It was over.

ALEGRA WATCHED Joe go. She knew he wouldn't be back, and, oddly, that was okay even if she felt something very similar to pain, but deeper and more blurred. It would be easier for her to do what she had to do without him there telling her she shouldn't do it, that it was futile. She wouldn't run into him. She wouldn't see him on the beach or in town. He'd avoid her and she would avoid him while she was here. She headed to her cottage and looked ahead, into the near future. Not back at a sad old house and a man who'd seen her at her worst ever since she'd stepped foot back on the island. Tomorrow night this would be over.

She went into the cottage and turned on her computer,

then her cell phone. And got to work. She didn't stop until it was dark outside and she could hear the sounds of the barbecue on the beach below the bluffs. She tuned out the noises and went back to work. Around midnight, she shut everything down and climbed into bed. She was exhausted, probably more from the emotional turmoil than anything physical. But despite that, sleep wouldn't come. She finally got up, went to get the cognac that was left and a snifter, then went back to bed.

She sat with her back against the headboard, sipped the cognac and tried to think about anything except what would take place the next night. She continued to hope the alcohol would blot out any dreams that might come when she finally fell asleep….

She awoke the next morning, curled in a ball on her side. She had a brief moment of satisfaction when she realized that if she'd dreamed, she couldn't remember any of it. But when she rolled over and started to sit up, pain exploded in her head. When she thought about last night, how she'd kept sipping until she fell asleep and how she'd done so on an empty stomach, no less, she knew the hangover was only what she deserved.

Finally, she swung her legs off the mattress and pushed herself to her feet. She needed water, lots of water. She retrieved two bottles from the minibar, drank one quickly, then the second more slowly.

With the half-empty bottle in her hand, she went in search of some aspirin. Finding a packet in a basket on the vanity by the sink, she swallowed two, then took a long, hot shower. By the time she emerged, she felt almost human.

She dressed in jeans and a deep red, heavy corduroy shirt. She ignored the computer which she'd shut down last night, but picked up the cell phone. Then she left the cottage and walked out into another clear, cold day. The sun was so bright she wished she had sunglasses. That made her laugh until pain darted through her head from the effort. Who would have thought she'd ever need sunglasses on Shelter Island?

The Bounty Festival was back in full gear, with laughter and music in the air. The main street, when she reached it, was car-free and blanketed with people, most in pirate costume. Everyone looked incredibly happy.

She headed down the street to find coffee and finally spotted a shop with remarkably few people inside. She went in, ordered a tall, black coffee and took a seat at a table by the window. When the doorbell chimed, she looked up and saw Joe's mother coming through the door. Before Alegra could look away, Christina Lawrence spotted her, smiled brightly at her, waved and called out, "I'm just here for my caffeine fix before the parade starts. Let me get it and we can talk for a bit before heading out for the celebration."

Before Alegra could say she was ready to leave, Christina was ordering her coffee, then coming across to the table with it. She sat opposite Alegra and proceeded to put four sugar packets in her cup. She smiled as she stirred. "Joe always says I like a little coffee with my sugar."

The woman was lovely and completely unpretentious, and after she sipped some coffee, she sat back with an, "Ah, I needed that." Alegra drank more of her own brew and when she grimaced at the ache still lingering behind her eyes, Christina said, "A bit too much of the grape?"

"Something like that," Alegra said. "But coffee sure helps."

"Amen," Christina breathed. "So, you know the parade's starting soon?"

That explained the car-free street. Must have been barricaded.

"You have to see it," Christina went on. "Most of the people in it are locals, and they make the floats and everything." She leaned forward. "I helped with the main float. Actually, when I was a lot younger, I was one of the serving wenches on the float." She grinned. "It was so much fun. That was the year I realized I loved Joe." The grin eased to a soft expression that touched her eyes. "A very good year all around."

"You grew up here?"

"Both of us did." She drank more coffee. "Then Joey of course, and now Alex. It's a wonderful circle of life, don't you think?"

She did. One that was very appealing, but one she'd never know. "It's good Joe brought Alex back here."

"I think so. Of course, the reasons were painful, but the outcome is what counts."

Painful? "I guess a divorce is never easy."

Christina looked at her blankly for a moment, then seemed to understand what she'd meant. "Oh, yes, of course, but that wasn't it. He and Jean had been divorced for a while when he made the decision. It seemed sudden, but I think the idea had been brewing in Joey's mind for some time. You see, he had a terrible fright and—"

"A fright?"

"Oh, yes, just the worst. Joey was at work when he got a call from the police. Alex had been at the park with his nanny and he'd disappeared." Alegra knew her shock was evident when Christina added quickly, "Oh, dear, no, Alex was fine. It turned out he'd just wandered off with some other kids, but Joey called to say he wanted to bring Alex back to the island to live. He didn't talk much about his decision, still doesn't. But I know he's really changed his priorities about a lot of things, especially about work."

"But he bought the newspaper."

"Oh, I think he did that because he likes writing and being in the mix, but there's little to no pressure, and he can make his own hours. He's not taking off on some assignment or pulling in all-nighters anymore."

Alegra heard a band starting up, and police were moving people off the street and onto the walkway.

Christina touched Alegra on the arm. "The parade's starting." She got to her feet. "I love it. Things like this make me really appreciate having this place to call home."

Alegra stood and picked up her coffee to take with her. "I need to go. I have to—"

"Yes, we need to get out there before the first band comes by, and if I know my Joe, he's fighting off the hordes to keep our spot," Christina said, apparently assuming Alegra was going with her.

Alegra, however, had no intention of standing in a suffocating crowd to see a parade. She'd go back to the Snug Harbor and wait out the day there. The ball was tonight. On the sidewalk, as Alegra was about to head back to the bed-and-breakfast, they ran into Joe, with Alex on his shoulders. Joe was smiling and Alex was bouncing with excitement.

"Dad's got a great spot," Joe said, before realizing, apparently, the woman inches from him was Alegra. His cheerful expression slipped a bit. "He's worried we won't get back before it starts."

"I ran in to Alegra in the coffee shop," Christina was saying in a voice loud enough to be heard over the band that was warming up out of sight. "I hope he's got a good spot for all of us."

Joe's eyes stayed on Alegra. "It's a good spot," he said, and glanced away to his mother. "Over by the park entrance, right by the statue."

"Perfect." Christina slipped her arm through Alegra's and tugged her with her, giving her no option except to go with her. "We don't want to miss a moment."

So Alegra went with Christina, with Joe and Alex right behind them. They found Joe Senior near the entry to the park, doing his best to keep a few square feet of sidewalk clear for the rest of his family. When he saw Alegra, he grinned at her. "You won't believe this parade," he said as his wife pulled Alegra into the cleared area.

Right then the band started in earnest, and Alex yelled, "It's here. It's here!"

Alegra looked up at the boy, instead of down the street the way everybody else was doing. Alex was flushed with excitement, his deep blue eyes bright with joy, and he clapped the same way his grandfather and father were clapping. Three generations of Lawrences watching the same parade. The thought made Alegra swallow the lump rising in her throat, and she quickly looked down the street at the approaching band.

Strains of "Stars and Stripes Forever" rang in the air as the band, made up of teenagers in bright red uniforms, earnestly played their instruments. A voice came over the loudspeakers. "The marching band from Shelter Island High School." People cheered and clapped and flashes went off.

Alegra would leave as soon as she could slip away without making a scene, but to do that, she had to stay at the back of their little group where Joe was until the time came.

Chapter Thirteen

A perfectly restored Model A Ford, carrying two men, brought up the rear of the band. "Ladies and gentlemen," the voice on the loudspeakers said, "our Mayor, Bill Foyle." The cheers rose. Then, "And our fire chief, Joe Armstrong." More cheers. At first Alegra stood back, just waiting for the moment she could leave, but the crowd surged forward and she had no choice but to go with it. She got on tiptoes to look down the street and saw the first float coming into view.

It looked like the crow's nest of an old ship, much like the gazebo in the park, and it held several men dressed like pirates. A live parrot was tethered to one man's shoulder. The others waved swords and pumped fists in the air, while the band changed to a rousing version of "Blow the Man Down." Jugglers, also dressed like pirates, danced around the float as it made its way down the street, juggling huge black balls, without dropping one of them. More floats came past, some simple, no more than flatbeds with club members on them, and some more complex. Then one all decorated with flowers came into sight. "Sonya Reyes, Miss Shelter Island," blared from the loudspeakers.

Alegra still wanted out of there, but as she turned, her arm hit Joe's. They both looked at each other, then amazingly, Joe smiled at her. "Fun, isn't it?" he called over the noise.

She looked away without answering, because at that moment, the lump in her throat wouldn't let her speak. Yes, it was all fun, and no kid should be sneaking away the morning after high school graduation. She bit her lip hard and turned back to the parade, but she didn't see anything except herself in the early-morning light heading for the ferry.

Christina moved closer to put an arm around her shoulders and whisper in her ear. "This is my float coming up," she said. "And take special note of the tree trunks. I did them. Also, the man dressed like a pirate is Sean Payne, a local artist. His work's really getting popular and they asked him to be old Bartholomew for the parade and at the ball tonight."

Alegra felt bile rise in her throat as Christina let her go, and she had to force herself to look at the street and the float coming into view. It was at least thirty feet long on a flatbed that had been decorated to look like a beach with palm trees and rocks and sand. A fake fire came out of a pile of stones, and pirates sat around it. One man stood, in costume, above them all, waving to the crowd with one hand and a large sword in the other. Sean Payne.

She stared at his tall, thin form, waiting for something to come besides this sense of dread, but there was nothing. He grinned at the crowds, waved, yelled, "Aye, matey!" at the top of his voice and seemed to be having a great time. The man was a stranger. There was no part of the boy left in him.

The crowd cheered and the band coming right after the float broke into a piece that she remembered from the past, "Bad, Bad Bartholomew," a song one of the music teachers at the high school had written years ago. "Isn't it great?" Christina called, twisting to look back at her and Joe and Alex.

"Yeah, Mom, just great," Joe said, and Alex bobbed his head in agreement.

Christina looked at Alegra. "If you don't have anything to do for dinner, come on over. We're having our pirate's meal." She grinned. "Meat and potatoes, and the meat, I have to warn you, is pretty bloody. It's a tradition with us, and I hate to break tradition."

If she let go, Alegra thought, she'd fall into this world of family and laughter and traditions. "Thanks," she managed to say to Christina, not accepting or refusing the invitation. She glanced up at Joe, intending to say she had to leave, but he was watching the parade. For a moment she allowed herself to just look at him. She saw the strong line of his jaw and the way his hair curled vaguely at the temples. She could see a pulse beating under his ear, a steady beat that, for a crazy minute, she was sure she could feel in her own body.

Quickly, she looked away. She just wanted not to be

where she was at that moment. She wouldn't let herself playact this way, pretending she was part of this, that she thought Sean looked great as Bartholomew. She eased away from the family, going back until people moved between her and Joe. Finally she broke free, and minutes later was in the parking lot of the bed-and-breakfast. Then she was at her cottage and opening the door.

As she closed it, she began to shake. All she could think of was Joe and Alex and their traditions and how they came home every day, day in and day out, to a perfect place. Of Sean smiling and making his grand entrance. Of Joe Senior and Christina smiling at each other. Then Joe by her side.

She closed her eyes tightly, taking deep breaths and telling herself over and over that none of this mattered. But even as she chanted the denial in her mind, she knew it wasn't true. No matter what she told herself, if she let go, it would all matter so very much to her. Especially Joe. He would matter more than life itself.

Her heart sank when the truth cut through her. She'd let him slip into her life and in the process become the part of it that made her feel alive. But it was impossible. Totally crazy. It was a weakness she hadn't known she had until she met him on the ferry. But a weakness she could control. When she left, she'd be changed, and she knew that the clean break she wanted from this place wasn't possible. She'd take some of this with her, and most of it would be what happened between her and Joe.

She just wasn't sure how she'd live like that, but she would. She'd lived through worse things and gone on.

She wouldn't even think about the loneliness hovering out there for her. She'd get past that, too. She'd work. She'd become more successful and somewhere, sometime, all this would fade away and be gone. She'd be in control again.

She crossed to the desk, hit the refresh button on the computer and her mail screen flashed to life. She counted six messages from Roz, but from the subject lines, she knew she could ignore them. She called Roz, however, to check that the fund-allocation request had been sent to the ball officials. Roz assured her it was all in place, and that the town officials would absolutely do as she wished. The lighthouse would be restored and fully operational.

"Thank you, Roz," Alegra said.

She hung up and headed into the bedroom. She tried to block out the noises from the street as she took out her bags and started to pack. She wanted to be ready to leave on the first ferry in the morning. She left out a shimmering silver dress and accessories she planned on wearing to the ball, her old T-shirt for sleeping, but packed everything else. She was reaching for her cosmetic bag when a knock sounded on the door. She headed to it and called, "Who's there?"

Nothing. She finally pulled the door open and knew she hadn't escaped at all. Joe stood there, and she was filled with both fear and joy. She knew the minute she faced him and met those eyes that she was very close to loving him.

"Why did you do that?" he asked.

She stared at him and wondered why she'd been stupid enough to think that she could control anything about Joe or her feelings for him as he moved past her into the cottage. She turned, letting the door shut, and he was a foot from her, facing her.

"Do what?" she managed.

"Disappear."

Damn it, the cottage felt so small! "I had to get back. I needed to…do things."

"Then why didn't you just say that and go?"

Because you were there, and all I wanted was for you to smile down at me and hold me to your side. The words never made it past her lips. "I'm sorry," she said.

"Mom thinks you're angry, that she said something that upset you."

"She didn't upset me," Alegra said. But that was a lie. Christina's talk about Joe, about having a home here, family traditions and the like had torn at Alegra, though she was certain the older woman hadn't suspected the impact her words had. "She just talked about…things."

Joe came closer. "What things?"

Oh, why lie? Alegra thought now. "You."

"What about me?"

"About you coming back here and making your home here."

Joe exhaled. "Then you know everything about me."

"No, I don't," she murmured.

"What more is there?"

"I still don't know how you could have just walked away from everything, just like that, and…"

"Give it all up?"

The blue of his eyes seemed almost black now. Dark and intense. She turned from his gaze to walk to the windows and look out. "Yes," she said. "How could you just walk away from all you'd worked for and come back to this place? I know it must have been awful when Alex disappeared, but to give up everything seems insane."

"I just wanted to come home," he said.

It was a simple explanation, yet the words made her realize what she didn't have, what she wanted. A home. But there was no such place for her. She closed her eyes. "So you left everything just to come home?"

"I didn't leave everything," he said in a low voice. "I have everything I want right here."

"Well, good for you," she muttered, and was shocked at the sarcasm in her tone. She turned from the window. He'd taken off his jacket and laid it on the couch back. He stood across the room, watching her, and she prayed she wouldn't lose control, although every nerve in her body was growing rawer and rawer. "You've got a place to come home to. You've got your family and everything's perfect for you. I'm happy for you, I really am."

As if on cue, she heard the music outside switch to "Home, Sweet Home." "Perfect," she muttered. "Just perfect."

Joe came closer, hesitated, then said in a low, rough voice, "Alegra, if you wanted to, you could have a home, too. You could have everything you ever wanted."

She glared at him. "I have everything I want," she insisted, but knew she didn't have anything at all.

"Do you?" he asked. He captured her face between his palms. "I don't."

"But…you…"

"I don't have you," he said.

THE ADMISSION surprised him. But it was true. He wanted her. He thought he could just walk away, that he'd go on and never look back again, but he'd been wrong. When he'd seen her with his mom, then watched her watching the parade, he'd known what a fool he'd been. It didn't matter what she did or didn't do. All that mattered was being with her.

As he held Alegra's face and looked into those amber eyes, Joe knew that just being with her wasn't the bottom line, either. He loved her. It had come quickly and hit him directly. It wasn't soft and peaceful, creeping up on him; it was unnerving and intense. It consumed him, made him ache. It stunned him to realize he'd never really been in love before. He'd never even come close.

"Oh, Joe," he heard her say and he didn't hesitate to lean forward and touch her lips with his. His love for her didn't come slowly and peacefully, it burst on him, filling him with need and desire, and when her arms lifted to circle his neck, when her breasts flattened against his chest, he didn't look back.

Her taste filled him, her heat seared through him, and he knew he'd waited his whole life for this woman. He lifted her and wrapped her legs around him and kissed her deeply. He carried her into the bedroom, the shadows soft with the drapes closed to the day outside. He lowered himself to the bed with her still against him, and he pushed at a suitcase, sending it and its contents to the floor in a heap.

He let her go only long enough to kick off his boots, then he was with her, twisting toward her in the mussed linen as her body arched toward his. He loved her touch on him, the way her hands worked their way under his shirt, and he wanted nothing more than to feel her bare skin. He fumbled with the buttons on her heavy shirt, and she fell back into the bed, not moving, her amber eyes never leaving his as he managed to undo the fasteners. He finally pushed the soft material aside, and there was no coyness in Alegra as he touched her breasts through the fine lace of her bra. She gasped and arched toward him, then threw her head back and closed her eyes.

He felt the tightening of her nipples under his fingers, and he lifted the lace, freeing her breasts. Then his lips took the place of his hands, and she trembled. He sucked and teased her nipples, until his own desire demanded he take off his jeans. When he eased back and off the bed, her eyes opened immediately and she whispered, "Please."

He quickly stripped off his jeans, shirt, then his briefs and went back to her. He helped Alegra tug off her jeans and panties, then tossed them into the shadows. She came to him, naked skin against naked skin, heat mingling with heat. He tasted her, working his way from her lips to her throat, to her breasts again, then to her stomach. Then lower. He heard her sharp intake of air as he touched her moist heat, and she cried out when his fingers entered her.

Suddenly, there was nothing but need. Hot, burning need. She was pulling him to her, and he got over her, between her legs, and touched her with his hardness. He tested her, then made himself say, "I want you."

She was under him, her breathing ragged, and she whispered, "Just love me."

It was the easiest request he'd ever fulfilled. He entered her, slowly and completely. Deep in her, he stopped, looked down at her, and as her hips lifted, he started to move. God help him, he loved her beyond reason. He loved the feel of her, the smell of her, the way she moved with him, the way she gave small gasps with each new level of feeling reached.

He loved the way her fingers dug into his shoulders, and the way her legs circled his hips, pulling him ever more deeply inside her. He loved the way she started to gasp, then arch and tremble. He loved the way his own cry of pleasure mingled with hers. In that moment, he really understood how two people could become one. One person. One need. One climax. He soared with it, never wanting it to end.

ALEGRA WAS VERY STILL in the shadows, feeling Joe against her side, his warm skin against hers, his arm around her, holding her to him. She listened to his even breathing and knew he was asleep. She was overwhelmed with what she'd done. She'd let everything that shouldn't have happened, happen. She let herself go to him, give herself to him and make love with him.

No, she'd simply let herself love him.

She was appalled at her total loss of control. Yet she'd wanted it more than she'd ever wanted anything in her life. She'd wanted to be loved and to love. She'd wanted to be so close to Joe that nothing separated them. And she had done that very thing. She'd let him in her, and she'd lost herself in feelings that were exquisitely beautiful and terrifying at the same time.

Now she didn't know what to do. How could she leave now? How could she walk away from Joe? Yet how could she *not* leave? She didn't belong here, even with Joe. She hadn't fit in here in the past. She wouldn't fit in now. She felt him stir, and she tensed, but then he sank back into sleep.

But she was wrong about him being asleep. "Awake?" he asked in a low murmur.

She thought of feigning sleep, but the moment his hand stroked her arm, then lowered to the curve of her hip, she couldn't suppress a sigh. "Yes," she whispered.

He shifted then, pushed himself up on his elbow to look down at her. "Good." She could see the smile on his lips in the dim light. "I'm awake, too." And his hand moved on her. He caressed her hip, her thigh, then pulled her leg up and over his. She trembled when he cupped her bottom in his hand, then touched her center. She gasped and closed her eyes at the feelings that seemed to come out of nowhere.

"Oh, Joe," she breathed, and pressed her lips to his chest. She found his nipple, teasing it with her tongue, and she heard him echo her gasp. She felt him tighten, then pressure against her stomach from his swell of desire. She thought about stopping, about saying, "We need to talk," but didn't, especially when he caught her around the waist with his hands and easily lifted her up and over him. She pressed her hands to the bed by his shoulders and felt him ease inside her as she lowered onto him.

No talking, not now. Later. Later. He moved in her, and she echoed those moves. She let the feelings flow through her, gave in to them. Joe carried her higher and higher, and was with her when she climaxed. His body tangled with hers, his mouth plundered hers, and her world narrowed to just the two of them. She clung to him, afraid to let go. Then she settled beside him, her leg over his, her arm around his waist, and his arm cradling her shoulders. She felt him press a kiss to her hair and heard his soft, "Thank you."

She closed her eyes tightly, and put off saying anything. She'd talk to him after the ball. After she was done. There had to be some way to make this work. Some way to keep this man in her life and close to her. Some way.

She was amazed that she actually slept. When she awoke, Joe was gone. In his place was a short note lying on the pillow that still held the indentation of his head. *Won't be gone long. Wait for me. We'll talk.* It was signed with a looping *J*.

She rolled back into the pillows and stared at the curtains over the windows. It was dark outside, she could tell, with no sun peeking through the crack where the panels met. She glanced at the bedside clock and saw it was after seven. The ball started at eight. She reached for the note Joe left, but there was no time on it. She had no idea when he'd left or how long he'd be.

She laid the note back on the pillow, then got out of bed. Yes, they'd talk. And she had no idea what either one would say. Loving Joe hadn't made her life any simpler, only more complicated, but she'd figure something out. She had to. They could find some arrangement both could live with. Because, one thing she knew, she wanted Joe in her life. She wanted to be with a man who made her feel as if she'd been waiting for his embrace her whole life.

She got out of bed, showered and quickly dressed for the ball in the silver, floor-length sheath, with thin jeweled straps at the shoulders and a scooped neckline. The back plunged to the small of her back. She caught her hair up and off her face with two diamond clips, then quickly applied makeup. All the while, she expected a knock on the door, to hear Joe call out to her. But by the time she was ready and had to leave, Joe still hadn't shown up.

She hurried into the bedroom, wrote a note of her own, saying she was at the ball and would be back as soon as she finished there. She hesitated, but didn't write what she wanted to, *Love, Alegra.* Instead she ended with, *Back soon. Alegra.*

She gathered up a small black evening bag and hurried out. She got to her car and headed to the Grace Mansion. She knew where it was and didn't have any trouble finding the road that cut off the main route and led to the jutting piece of land that descendants of Bartholomew Grace owned.

She rounded a curve on the narrow road and came face-to-face with the huge entry gates to the property. Rough stones formed pillars on both sides almost twenty feet high, and wrought-iron gates with a fancy *B* on one and an equally fancy *G* on the other were hinged to the pillars. There was a numeric pad on the left for guests, but on this evening, a man in full formal attire greeted everyone at the entrance. He scanned her invitation, then nodded to her and said, "Please, enter the Grace estate."

She had never been beyond the gates in her life, but what she found inside pretty much lived up to her fantasies about the place. The main house was high on a bluff. Outside lights exposed a structure of rock and wood that bordered on being a castle, yet looked almost crude in its construction. It had light pouring out every window of its three stories. Several chimneys reached into the dark sky, smoke curling out of every one of them.

She followed the winding drive to the house, passing two side routes that were labeled with signs that read, respectively, Employee Entrance, and Utilities. At the house she surrendered her car to a valet who appeared as soon as she stopped by steep stone steps leading to the entry. She didn't pause to look around, but hurried up the steps and through open wooden doors.

The central foyer of the house was as big as her apartment in New York. Twin staircases wound to the left and right. The walls in here were stone, also, polished and mellow. A huge iron chandelier cast soft light through the area, and the floor, polished pink marble, was oddly out of place. It was as if the idea of luxury was embraced only on the floor. The rest was rough and, although expansive, without refinement.

A man in tails approached her, asked for her name, then proceeded to show her through a massive archway directly ahead and under the upper balconies. She stepped down into another large space, with the same pink marble flooring, but with intricately detailed dark wood on all the walls and the high, coved ceiling. An orchestra was in an alcove to the right, mostly strings playing a waltz, and a number of couples were in the middle of the space dancing.

She figured there were already about a hundred people at the ball, and she was right on time. People around here obviously didn't believe in being fashionably late. She took an offered flute of champagne and was introduced to Harry Tarver, the name she recognized from the forms she'd filled in for the donation. He was tall and bald, and his welcome was effusive when he found out who she was.

She begged off dancing with him, then asked when the ceremony would start for the contributors, because she really didn't want to spend a lot of time at the ball. The man assured her the ceremony would start within the hour. She thanked him, then moved to the back of the room and a series of French doors that showed the magnificent view from the property.

The night was unusually clear, and stars were visible. She could see the lights from the mainland far off in the distance. If the lighthouse had been working, she'd be seeing its light sweeping back and forth in the night. Well, that would happen soon.

She was startled when a hand touched her shoulder. She turned to see Joe Senior. The older man was dressed in a tux and grinning at her. "You made it and you look lovely." He held his hand out to her. "Give this old guy a treat and dance with me before Joey comes back and keeps you all to himself?"

Chapter Fourteen

Alegra looked past Joe Senior and saw Christina near the middle of the room dancing with a young guy who looked pretty awkward waltzing. Christina smiled at her, waved, and Alegra waved back. Why hadn't she thought they might be here? She hadn't even considered them standing there when she made her announcement. She let Joe Senior lead her to the dance floor.

He was a smooth dancer and easy to follow, which was good because she was having trouble focusing, knowing Joe Junior would probably be there soon. "You missed a great pirate meal," the man said. "Then again, so did Joey."

That made her miss her step slightly, but she recovered. "He didn't make it for dinner?"

"We're used to that. He gets tied up here and there and really isn't good at following any sort of schedule." She hoped this wasn't Joe Senior's subtle way of telling her he knew they'd been together.

"I was busy," she mumbled, almost choking on the words.

"We figured as much," he said evenly, and she missed her step again. "You know, you haven't changed very much."

She stopped. "Excuse me?"

He smiled wryly and his blue eyes narrowed on her. "You are very much all right, aren't you?"

She stared at him, but before she could figure out what had just happened, someone touched her shoulder, and Joe Senior's smile grew. "Joey! There you are. And here's Alegra."

With that, the older man let her go, and she had only a glimpse of Joe in a tux before she found herself in his arms. She snuggled into his chest and felt his heart beating against her cheek. The sense of rightness she felt made her smile. She moved easily and remembered how they'd moved when they made love.

Finally he spoke. "I thought you were waiting for me at the cottage." She felt the rumble of the words in his chest.

"I waited, but it got late and I had to be here," she said against the fine material of his tux.

He held her more tightly against him, and all but stopped moving to the music as he whispered in her ear, "I thought you'd let this all go."

The good feelings were starting to fade. "I never said I was, did I?"

"No, but I thought…" He sighed roughly, then said earnestly, "Come with me, now. We'll just walk away and keep going until we're alone and can talk and figure out a better way."

They'd stopped dancing completely, and his hold on her was feeling more restrictive than comforting. As if Joe had read her mind, he eased his embrace and she was able to move back enough to look up at him. "I can't just walk away, not now, not after all of this," she said. "We can talk later."

He glanced around, then back at her. "Come on," he said, and led her across the dance floor. Just as a new piece started, they reached the French doors. Joe pushed the nearest one open and ushered her out onto an expansive stone terrace. Old gas lamps flickered along the wall, and the night was cold. But Alegra didn't notice much more than the fact that Joe had released her arm and now stood a distance from her, his expression tense.

"Joe, you can't think I'd just forget doing all this just because we…" She bit her lip, not wanting to diminish in any way their exquisite lovemaking earlier.

"You're still going to go through with this revenge?"

"I have to," she said again, with a touch of desperation in her voice.

"Why? You are who you are, and you can be anyone you want to be. You've proven that. But you don't have to do this."

If she could only think of what to say to recapture their closeness, yet not sacrifice what she'd come here to do. "I told you how important this is to me."

Joe came closer, inches from her. "Alegra, I'm begging you. Let it go and leave here with me now." His voice was rough.

"You'll come with me?" she asked.

"Yes, we'll go back to your place or my house, or even to the beach. We can talk and—"

She cut him off. "Will you leave the island with me?"

The question hung between them, unanswered, for what seemed like an eternity. Finally Joe shook his head. "This is my home, but it can be your home, too."

Her heart broke. "It never was my home," she whispered. "It can't ever be my home. I hate it here. I can't wait to leave." Her voice got louder and more hysterical with each word. She stopped herself by putting a hand over her mouth. She stared at Joe, then slowly lowered her hand. She took a breath and said sorrowfully, "It can't work, can it."

"No," he murmured.

Nothing felt right now, nothing fit, and when she heard the announcer say that the donation ceremony was beginning, she couldn't look away from Joe. "I…I need to go inside," she said.

Joe moved so close she could feel his body heat. "I know you do," he said in a voice that sounded so much like pity she wanted to scream. It was as if he'd said she was a fool but go and do what she thought she had to do. She wanted to tell him that if he cared about her, he'd back her in this, try to understand, not pity her. God, she hated that! The pain she felt now was far beyond anything Sean had inflicted on her years ago.

Names were being read off, then her name was called, and Joe didn't move. She brushed a hand over her face. "That's me," she said, and moved to go around him, leaving him behind, to go into the ballroom and back to her life she'd chosen.

But then he had her by her shoulders, and turned her to look at him. "Believe it or not," he said, "I wish you everything you ever wanted in this life." With that, he pressed his mouth to hers briefly, then drew back and walked inside, leaving her out there alone. On stiff legs, she followed, not sure if she was going after him or the revenge she so wanted.

But as she stepped into the ballroom, the man on the podium by the orchestra said over the microphone, "Ladies and gentlemen, Alegra Reynolds." They all turned in her direction, and in the blur of faces, the only one she saw with any clarity was Joe's. He was watching her from the other side of the room, then he disappeared through the large archway. The crowd began to applaud, and an attendant reached her, took her by the arm and murmured, "Let me escort you."

Accompanied by him and the applause, she climbed onto the small stage with Mayor Foyle. He beamed at her. From a small card in his hand, he read off who she was professionally and that she had made a donation with the stipulation that it be used to restore the lighthouse and keep it in working order. When he read the amount, there was a collective gasp from the audience, followed by a crescendo of applause and shouts of approval.

The mayor turned to her, said, "We all thank you for caring enough about our island to make it a better place,

Ms. Reynolds," then he stepped away from the microphone, letting her take his place.

She gripped the microphone stand tightly, at a loss, momentarily, for how to begin. She looked out at the sea of people, then saw Joe Senior and Christina smiling at her, and Christina giving her a thumbs-up. Alegra looked away from them as she finally understood, unnerved when she realized Joe and Christina knew who she was. She cleared her throat and began.

"My name is Alegra Reynolds." She paused. "You all knew me years ago as…"

She stopped, unable to continue with the speech she'd planned, the speech where she told them she was Al Peterson, daughter of the town drunk who no one ever imagined would make anything of herself. She stood there, waiting, but the words wouldn't come. She knew in that moment that nothing she could say or do here was going to replace the emptiness inside her, the emptiness that had settled into a living thing when Joe disappeared from view. She'd never felt like that in her life, not even at the worst of times when she was a child.

She turned to the mayor, then back to the crowd and could barely focus on anyone at all. Joe was the only person around here who knew who she really was, and suddenly that was all that mattered. He knew, and Joe hadn't left because of what she was or what she'd done before, but because she was asking him to back her in this insane quest for revenge and recognition. In that moment, she realized she didn't need it. She managed to say, "I'd love to see the old lighthouse in working order. When I was growing up, its light was a beacon of hope for me, and perhaps it can be the same for some of you."

That was it. That was all she was going to say. She absorbed the thunderous applause, but knew it meant little to her. She didn't need to see their faces drop with surprise and shock when she threw her real identity in their faces, when she told them they were applauding little Al Peterson. She didn't need to see their embarrassment or hear any apologies, sincere or otherwise. She'd come to the island for one thing—to put Al Peterson to rest and leave without regret. She knew then that she'd put the little girl in her to rest, and wasn't quite sure when that had happened. But if she left now, she would have regrets for the rest of her life.

JOE LEFT THE MANSION with the applause for Alegra echoing in his ears. He went quickly down the stone steps, but didn't wave the valet over to get his car for him. Instead, he headed to the north end of the house and onto a trail he'd gone on many times when he'd been a kid playing with Ethan Grace, a school friend. It led to a lookout cut in the rocky bluffs where Bartholomew Grace once used his spyglass to search the horizon for his enemies.

He went to the safety railing and leaned with both hands on the cold iron, then bowed his head and exhaled. For a short flash of time he'd thought he'd found something so rare that he never would have guessed it existed until it had existed for him. His love for a woman. But it wasn't enough—Alegra needed so much more. Why had he thought his love *would* be enough? He straightened and raked his fingers through his hair, feeling more alone than he ever had.

He could still hear the sounds of celebration from the mansion, and he hoped that Alegra was getting everything she wanted, everything she needed. He stared out across the sound, over the glimmer of starlight on the black waters, at the halo of light from the city on the mainland, and felt as if he was looking at another world. Alegra's world.

"Joe?"

He thought he'd imagined her saying his name at first, but when it was repeated and sounded nearer, he knew it was real. As real as the woman he turned to face. Alegra.

He didn't mean to speak right then, especially words that came out with more than a touch of harshness. "Now you have it all, Alegra."

She moved closer and the silver of her dress shimmered in the starlight. Her blond hair was a cloud around her shadowed face, and she looked delicate and vulnerable. "No, I don't," she said, stopping within two feet of him.

"Humiliation and revenge weren't enough for you?" he asked, motioning with one hand toward the mansion.

She didn't answer that, but said softly, "Do you remember the moment when you were in New York and you knew you had to come back here?"

He couldn't think about the past now, about anything except how much he loved her. But he nodded. "Yes."

"It's called an epiphany, I think. Of course, you're the human dictionary. You'd know all about that."

"Epiphany," he repeated, never taking his eyes off of her. "A sudden moment of comprehension or perception of reality from an intuitive realization."

"I knew you'd know what it meant," she said in a voice barely above a whisper. "I never really knew about that sort of thing until the moment I had one."

"Telling people who you really are was your epiphany?"

"No, not even close. I think my epiphany happened earlier in the day." He saw her press her hands together in front of her, almost as if she was praying. "When I got up there and saw everyone, including your mom and dad. They know, don't they?" He simply nodded.

She laughed, a shaky sound in the night air. "Stupid, huh? All that time and energy, and it ended up you were right all along."

Joe found he could barely breathe waiting for her to say more. "And?" he finally said.

He heard her inhale as she lifted her face to him. "And? I'm not sure."

"What aren't you sure of?"

"What I have to do."

"About what?" he asked tensely.

She stared at him. "About you."

"What about me?"

"You aren't making this easy, are you?" she asked.

"Life isn't easy, Alegra," he said. "But it's your life, your choices."

"You're right," she said softly. "It's my life and my

choice is…" Her voice faded off in the cold air, and he saw her tremble. But he didn't dare touch her. If he did, he wouldn't let go.

"What do you choose, Alegra Reynolds?"

She came closer, and her features were exposed to him. He saw the way her mouth was pressed together, and the fine line between her eyes. "I…I choose you," she said.

"For how long?"

She blinked, then reached out slowly and pressed her hand to his chest right over his heart. He was quite certain she could feel the way it was hammering against his ribs. "For as long as you'll have me."

He wanted to believe her. Desperately. Still, he held back. "My life is here," he said simply.

She lifted her hand to touch his lips with the tips of her fingers. "Joe, I no longer blame this island. Yes, some people were cruel to me, but now I can forgive them. I let the anger and resentment I've been carrying all these years fill the empty spaces in me. When you touched me, I began to see how wrong that was. Empty spaces need to be filled with love, not hate. Now *you* fill those spaces. For the first time ever, I feel I've come home."

He reached for her, pulling her into an embrace. He had another epiphany. Home was where the people he loved were. And it all centered on this woman in his arms. He could leave here, but as long as she and Alex were with him, he'd be home. Really home.

They stood this way for some time, both reveling in the wondrous moment of discovery. When Joe lowered his head and kissed her, when she circled his neck with her arms and asked him to come back to the cottage with her, the wondrous moment didn't end. It had just begun.

Epilogue

The festival had been over for two weeks before Joe and Alegra told his family about their plans for the future. They'd kept it all to themselves, wanting time without the intrusion of others. They announced their engagement and their desire to marry quickly in a small ceremony. They were voted down, at least on their wish for a small wedding. Christina thought a wedding near Christmas would be perfect. Lots of red velvet and green ribbons. Alegra didn't care, as long as they were married and were a family before the new year began.

When Alegra's cell phone rang, the day they'd announced they were getting married, three pairs of eyes at the dinner table in the Lawrence bungalow turned to her. Alex liked the tone she'd loaded on it, a version of "Home, Sweet Home." It was Christina who smiled and said, "Tell Roz hi from all of us and we can't wait to meet her next week." Joe had gone to the newspaper office just before dinner, saying something about the new printing press acting up, and that he'd be back soon.

Alegra saw the LED readout and didn't recognize the number. She flipped it open. "Hello?"

"It's me," Joe said, and the sound of his voice gave her pleasure.

She smiled. He was actually using his new cell phone. "What's going on?"

"I'm coming to get you, but just tell Mom and Dad that I need you to help me out for a bit."

"You need my help?"

His low chuckle came over the line. "Absolutely. I need your help...*really* need it," he said, his voice lowering. She felt a thrill go through her.

"I'd be glad to help," she said, and he chuckled again. "When?"

"Come out the front door, walk to the road and I'm waiting in the truck at the end of the driveway. I don't want them to see me there, or they'll think of something they want me to do."

"Okay, no problem," she said, more than aware of the others pretending to concentrate on their food while they listened.

"I love you," he whispered roughly.

"Same to you," she responded softly.

"Okay, get going," Joe said, then hung up.

She flipped the phone shut and laid it on the table by her half-finished dinner of pot roast and carrots. "That was Joe," she said, looking at no one specifically. "He needs some help with...things." She got to her feet and smoothed the oversized white shirt she was wearing with jeans. "I'm not sure how long this is going to take."

"Anything we can do to help?" Joe Senior asked.

"Joe," Christina said, "I'm sure if Joey wanted our help, he would have called us." She smiled at Alegra. "Go ahead," she said, making a sweeping motion with her hand. "Go and help Joey and try to get some time to celebrate." She did all but wink at her knowingly.

Alegra leaned down to Alex in his high chair. "I'll be back in time to read you more out of your book," she said.

The little boy grinned and unexpectedly kissed her cheek. It stunned her, and she blinked at him. "I love you," she said, and meant it with all her heart.

She hurried through the house and out into the night. She jogged down the driveway, and saw the old truck idling on the road and ran to it. Climbing in, she buckled up and said, "You'll never guess what happened!" She reached for his hand.

"What now?"

"Alex, he…he kissed me when I was leaving."

Joe squeezed her fingers. "He's really taken to you."

"I love him," she whispered, a bit surprised at how unsteady her voice was becoming.

Joe seemed to understand and pulled her hand to his thigh, resting it there with his. "I'd say that for someone who's never thought much about kids, you've had a real victory."

They hadn't known each other all that long, just a few weeks, but so much had happened in that short amount of time. Kids had barely been spoken of, except for her to assure Joe that she wanted to do the best by Alex that she could. Now she knew that her love for Joe simply spread to his son. It was amazing to her. "I never thought I liked children, actually, but you know, things change."

He lifted her hand and kissed her knuckles. "Amen to that."

"I haven't thought much about it, but maybe…" She bit her lip, knowing what she wanted to say, but shocking herself with the fact that she really meant it. "A child shouldn't be an only child." She was, and Joe was, and he'd mentioned once that, like her, he'd have loved a sibling. "Alex is great, but maybe he should have a brother or sister?"

Joe was silent as he put the truck in gear and drove off. He turned into a driveway just past the old lighthouse area. Not a word was spoken as they drove under a canopy of pines, then into a place where the ruins of an old stone house had stood when she was a child. She used to play games of make-believe there, pretending the place was her very own house, where she slept and ate and made beautiful things, undisturbed by her drunken father.

Joe slowed as they broke free of the trees and she saw that a new house had been built on the spot, a comfortable-looking bungalow with a bottom half of stone and a top floor of clapboard. She saw lights on in the lower floor, and in the illumination of the truck's headlights, she saw smoke curling out of one of two chimneys.

Joe hadn't let go of her, and as soon as he stopped by the stone steps that led up to a wraparound porch, he turned to her. "Did you mean that?" he asked. "About a child, another child?"

She wasn't sure how to respond. He'd told her he'd

never wanted kids, though Alex had come to mean the world to him. But maybe he never wanted more. "I just thought…" she began, "maybe, in the future, we could…" She bit her bottom lip. "Are we getting out?" she asked, suddenly wanting to breathe cold air.

She opened the door and climbed out. Almost before she was on the ground, Joe was there, right in front of her. She looked around. "Why are we here?" she asked.

"It's for sale, and I have the key. The lighthouse is close enough that you can sit on the porch and watch the light at night." He didn't touch her. "I thought it sounded like a good idea if we bought it, if you like it."

He'd skipped right past the talk of a child, and so she let it go. What made him happy, made her happy. It was that simple. "I like it very much," she whispered.

He exhaled, then his hands framed her face and he was so close she thought she could hear the beat of his heart. "And about children," he started, but she put her forefinger to his lips and spoke quickly.

"It's just an idea. If you don't want to have more kids, that's okay. Alex is terrific. An only child is okay."

He pulled her against him and wrapped her in a hug. "I thought you wouldn't want children," he said, his voice muffled against her hair.

"I want yours," she said simply.

"Oh, God," he whispered. "I was so sure you wouldn't want more kids." He kissed her quickly. "I thought…"

She felt her heart leap in her breast. "And I thought you wouldn't want more."

"There's so much to learn about you," he said,

tasting her lips again, then pulling back to look at her. "So very much."

"And we've got a lifetime," she said.

Joe picked her up in his arms and carried her to the door. He managed to open it, and then strode with her into the great room, empty of furniture, but with polished wood floors and coved ceilings. He kept walking down a short hallway. He turned into what had to be the master bedroom. It was as empty, except for a stone fireplace to one side with a fire burning in it, and a pallet of pillows and blankets on the floor in front of it.

He crossed to the pallet and they were on them together, and that's when she saw the painting propped on the heavy mantel over the fireplace. It was her light-house. "Oh, Joe," she whispered, "I love this place."

"I love you," he uttered and started to undo her clothes. She quickly did the same for him, and soon they were naked in front of the fire, turning into each other's arms.

He kissed her neck, nuzzling into her heat. "We'll buy it," he murmured as he shifted and poised his body over hers. She thrilled to the moment he entered her, when she felt totally complete and at home. He touched her, kissed her, and moved in her. Their hips matched each other's actions, and a torrent of sensations flooded through her. She felt every contact of his skin with hers, heard every breath he took, and matched his own breathless gasp in their climax.

They fell together into a soft place of completion, and held onto each other as she tasted the saltiness of his skin, then ran her hand down his flat stomach.

"This is wonderful," she murmured against his chest. "No people, no work, no—"

"Cell phone?" he asked. "I left mine in the truck."

She laughed. "Well, I left mine at your parents'. Do you think your mom'll answer it if it rings?"

He pressed a kiss to her forehead. "She'll answer it and tell Roz how to run the business."

Alegra laughed again and felt freer and happier than she ever had. "It will be fun when Roz shows up here later."

He pushed up on his elbow, looked down at her, then gently eased a strand of hair off her forehead. "She's coming here?"

"Of course," she murmured, catching his hand to pull it down to her naked breast. "She'll be here for the wedding, but I also need her to learn more about the business, help me set up an office here. I want her to do more of the day-to-day business, take over a lot of my duties."

He cupped her bare breast in his hand. "Leaving you free for…" He gave a crooked smile.

She trembled at the intensity of her feelings for Joe. "Lovemaking. I want to make love with you forever."

He teased her nipple between his thumb and forefinger and said, "I do love your priorities."

Homecoming. It rang in her every time they were together, every time she saw him walk into a room, every time she heard his voice on the phone. Every time he made love to her. She was Alegra, and Joe Lawrence loved her. She was home.

* * * * *

Mediterranean Nights

Join the guests and crew of Alexandra's Dream,
*the newest luxury ship to set sail on the
romantic Mediterranean, as they experience
the glamorous world of cruising.*

*A new Harlequin continuity series
begins in June 2007 with*
FROM RUSSIA, WITH LOVE
by Ingrid Weaver

*Marina Artamova books a cabin on the luxurious
cruise ship* Alexandra's Dream, *when she finds out
that her orphaned nephew and his adoptive father are
aboard. She's determined to be reunited with the
boy...but the romantic ambience of the ship and
her undeniable attraction to a man she considers
her enemy are about to interfere with her quest!*

Turn the page for a sneak preview!

Piraeus, Greece

"THERE SHE IS, Stefan. *Alexandra's Dream*." David Anderson squatted beside his new son and pointed at the dark blue hull that towered above the pier. The cruise ship was a majestic sight, twelve decks high and as long as a city block. A circle of silver and gold stars, the logo of the Liberty Cruise Line, gleamed from the swept-back smokestack. Like some legendary sea creature born for the water, the ship emanated power from every sleek curve—even at rest it held the promise of motion. "That's going to be our home for the next ten days."

The child beside him remained silent, his cheeks working in and out as he sucked furiously on his thumb. Hair so blond it appeared white ruffled against his forehead in the harbor breeze. The baby-sweet scent unique to the very young mingled with the tang of the sea.

"Ship," David said. "Uh, *parakhod*."

From beneath his bangs, Stefan looked at the

Alexandra's Dream. Although he didn't release his thumb, the corners of his mouth tightened with the beginning of a smile.

David grinned. That was Stefan's first smile this afternoon, one of only two since they had left the orphanage yesterday. It was probably because of the boat—according to the orphanage staff, the boy loved boats, which was the main reason David had decided to book this cruise. Then again, there was a strong possibility the smile could have been a reaction to David's attempt at pocket-dictionary Russian. Whatever the cause, it was a good start.

The liaison from the adoption agency had claimed that Stefan had been taught some English, but David had yet to see evidence of it. David continued to speak, positive his son would understand his tone even if he couldn't grasp the words. "This is her maiden voyage. Her first trip, just like this is our first trip, and that makes it special." He motioned toward the stage that had been set up on the pier beneath the ship's bow. "That's why everyone's celebrating."

The ship's official christening ceremony had been held the day before and had been a closed affair, with only the cruise-line executives and VIP guests invited, but the stage hadn't yet been disassembled. Banners bearing the blue and white of the Greek flag of the ship's owner, as well as the Liberty circle of stars logo, draped the edges of the platform. In the center, a group of musicians and a dance troupe dressed in traditional white folk costumes performed for the benefit of the

Alexandra's Dream's first passengers. Their audience was in a festive mood, snapping their fingers in time to the music while the dancers twirled and wove through their steps.

David bobbed his head to the rhythm of the mandolins. They were playing a folk tune that seemed vaguely familiar, possibly from a movie he'd seen. He hummed a few notes. "Catchy melody, isn't it?"

Stefan turned his gaze on David. His eyes were a striking shade of blue, as cool and pale as a winter horizon and far too solemn for a child not yet five. Still, the smile that hovered at the corners of his mouth persisted. He moved his head with the music, mirroring David's motion.

David gave a silent cheer at the interaction. Hopefully, this cruise would provide countless opportunities for more. "Hey, good for you," he said. "Do you like the music?"

The child's eyes sparked. He withdrew his thumb with a pop. *"Moozika!"*

"Music. Right!" David held out his hand. "Come on, let's go closer so we can watch the dancers."

Stefan grasped David's hand quickly, as if he feared it would be withdrawn. In an instant his budding smile was replaced by a look close to panic.

Did he remember the car accident that had killed his parents? It would be a mercy if he didn't. As far as David knew, Stefan had never spoken of it to anyone. Whatever he had seen had made him run so far from the crash that the police hadn't found him until the next day. The event had traumatized him to the extent that he hadn't uttered a word until his fifth week at the orphanage. Even now he seldom talked.

David sat back on his heels and brushed the hair from Stefan's forehead. That solemn, too-old gaze locked with his, and for an instant, David felt as if he looked back in time at an image of himself thirty years ago.

He didn't need to speak the same language to understand exactly how this boy felt. He knew what it meant to be alone and powerless among strangers, trying to be brave and tough but wishing with every fiber of his being for a place to belong, to be safe, and most of all for someone to love him….

He knew in his heart he would be a good parent to Stefan. It was why he had never considered halting the adoption process after Ellie had left him. He hadn't balked when he'd learned of the recent claim by Stefan's spinster aunt, either; the absentee relative had shown up too late for her case to be considered. The adoption was meant to be. He and this child already shared a bond that went deeper than paperwork or legalities.

A seagull screeched overhead, making Stefan start and press closer to David.

"That's my boy," David murmured. He swallowed hard, struck by the simple truth of what he had just said.

That's my *boy*.

"I can't be patient, Rudolph. I'm not going to stand by and watch my nephew get ripped from his country and his roots to live on the other side of the world."

Rudolph hissed out a slow breath. "Marina, I don't like the sound of that. What are you planning?"

"I'm going to talk some sense into this American kidnapper."

"No. Absolutely not. No offence, but diplomacy is not your strong suit."

"Diplomacy be damned. Their ship's due to sail at five o'clock."

"Then you wouldn't have an opportunity to speak with him even if his lawyer agreed to a meeting."

"I'll have ten days of opportunities, Rudolph, since I plan to be onboard that ship."

* * * * *

*Follow Marina and David as they join forces
to uncover the reason behind little Stefan's unusual
silence, and the secret behind the death of his parents....*

*Look for FROM RUSSIA, WITH LOVE by
Ingrid Weaver
in stores June 2007.*

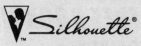

Silhouette®

Romantic
SUSPENSE

**Sparked by Danger,
Fueled by Passion.**

*This month and every month look for
four new heart-racing romances
set against a backdrop of suspense!*

Available in June 2007

Shelter from the Storm
by **RaeAnne Thayne**

A Little Bit Guilty
(Midnight Secrets miniseries)
by **Jenna Mills**

Mob Mistress
by **Sheri WhiteFeather**

A Serial Affair
by **Natalie Dunbar**

Available wherever you buy books!

Visit Silhouette Books at www.eHarlequin.com   SRS0507

REQUEST YOUR FREE BOOKS!
2 FREE NOVELS PLUS 2
FREE GIFTS!

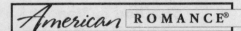

Heart, Home & Happiness!

YES! Please send me 2 FREE Harlequin American Romance® novels and my 2 FREE gifts. After receiving them, if I don't wish to receive any more books, I can return the shipping statement marked "cancel." If I don't cancel, I will receive 4 brand-new novels every month and be billed just $4.24 per book in the U.S., or $4.99 per book in Canada, plus 25¢ shipping and handling per book and applicable taxes, if any*. That's a savings of close to 15% off the cover price! I understand that accepting the 2 free books and gifts places me under no obligation to buy anything. I can always return a shipment and cancel at any time. Even if I never buy another book from Harlequin, the two free books and gifts are mine to keep forever.

154 HDN EEZK   354 HDN EEZV

Name	(PLEASE PRINT)
Address	Apt. #
City	State/Prov. Zip/Postal Code

Signature (if under 18, a parent or guardian must sign)

Mail to the **Harlequin Reader Service®:**
IN U.S.A.: P.O. Box 1867, Buffalo, NY 14240-1867
IN CANADA: P.O. Box 609, Fort Erie, Ontario L2A 5X3

Not valid to current Harlequin American Romance subscribers.

Want to try two free books from another line?
Call 1-800-873-8635 or visit www.morefreebooks.com.

* Terms and prices subject to change without notice. NY residents add applicable sales tax. Canadian residents will be charged applicable provincial taxes and GST. This offer is limited to one order per household. All orders subject to approval. Credit or debit balances in a customer's account(s) may be offset by any other outstanding balance owed by or to the customer. Please allow 4 to 6 weeks for delivery.

Your Privacy: Harlequin is committed to protecting your privacy. Our Privacy Policy is available online at www.eHarlequin.com or upon request from the Reader Service. From time to time we make our lists of customers available to reputable firms who may have a product or service of interest to you. If you would prefer we not share your name and address, please check here.

SPECIAL EDITION™

COMING IN JUNE

HER LAST
FIRST DATE

by *USA TODAY* bestsellling author
SUSAN MALLERY

After one too many bad dates, Crissy Phillips
finally swore off men. Recently widowed,
pediatrician Josh Daniels can't risk losing his
heart. With an intense attraction pulling them
together, will their fear keep them apart?
Or will one wild night change everything…?

**Sometimes the unexpected
is the best news of all….**

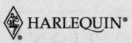

HARLEQUIN®

American ROMANCE®

COMING NEXT MONTH

#1165 SUMMER LOVIN' by Marin Thomas, Laura Marie Altom and Ann Roth

This year, celebrating the Fourth of July in Silver Cliff, Colorado, is going to be special. There's an all-year high school reunion taking place before the school building gets torn down. As old flames find each other and new romances begin, this season this small town is looking like the perfect place for some summer lovin'!

#1166 THE COWGIRL'S CEO by Pamela Britton

Barrel-racing star Caroline Sheppard wants only one thing: to win the NFR, the Super Bowl of rodeos. But she can't get there without help from millionaire businessman Tyler Harrison. And his sponsorship comes with strings attached. But even if Caro wants to turn him down, her heart, as Ty is about to learn, is as big as the Wyoming sky....

#1167 THE MAN FOR MAGGIE by Lee McKenzie

Having distanced himself from his wealthy family, Nick Durrance started his own construction business, and now pretty much keeps to himself. But Maggie Meadowcroft sees something special in the man and decides to work some magic on him to see if she can't reconnect him with his family and friends. But when he starts falling for Maggie, things get really interesting!

#1168 HIS ONLY WIFE by Cathy McDavid

Aubrey Stuart is reluctant to get involved with hotshot firefighter Gage Raintree. She loved him once, but now her life and her job as a nurse is in Tucson, far away from the small town of Blue Ridge. At the end of the summer she will have to leave—is the persistent Gage going to let her?

www.eHarlequin.com